THE RO

"The room of the title
space station built by an unknown intelligence; those unfortunate enough to venture into it disappear, die, or both. The station and the Room become an object of obsession and an almost religious devotion for those who search for the key to its mysteries. ... It's got a fascinating air of menace..."

—*SF Gospel*

Praise for
DIVING INTO THE WRECK, THE NOVEL

"This is classic sci-fi, a well-told tale of dangerous exploration. The first-person narration makes the reader an eyewitness to the vast, silent realms of deep space, where even the smallest error will bring disaster. Compellingly human and technically absorbing, the suspense builds to fevered intensity, culminating in an explosive yet plausible conclusion."

—*RT Book Reviews Top Pick*

"Rusch delivers a page-turning space adventure while contemplating the ethics of scientists and governments working together on future tech."

—*Publisher's Weekly*

"Rusch's handling of the mystery and adventure is stellar, and the whole tale proves quite e

Also by

Kristine Kathryn Rusch

Alien Influences
The End of The World (novella)
The Retrieval Artist Series

The Diving Universe:

Novellas

Diving into the Wreck
The Room of Lost Souls
Becalmed
Becoming One with the Ghosts
Stealth
Strangers at the Room of Lost Souls
The Spires of Denon

Novels

Diving into the Wreck
City of Ruins
Boneyards
The Diving Omnibus, Volume One
Skirmishes (September 2013)

The ROOM of LOST SOULS

A DIVING UNIVERSE NOVELLA

KRISTINE KATHRYN RUSCH

WMG PUBLISHING

The Room of Lost Souls

Published 2013 by WMG Publishing
www.wmgpublishing.com
First published in *Asimov's SF Magazine*, April/May 2008

Cover design by Allyson Longueira/WMG Publishing
ISBN-13: 978-0-615-79020-6
ISBN-10: 0-615-79020-8

The ROOM of LOST SOULS

A DIVING UNIVERSE NOVELLA

1

The old spacer's bar on Longbow Station is the only bar there that doesn't have a name. No name, no advertising across the door or the back wall, no cute little logos on the magnetized drinking cups. The door is recessed into a grungy wall that looks like it's temporary due to construction.

To get in, you need one of two special chips. The first is hand-held—given by the station manager after careful consideration. The second is built into your ID. You get that one if you're a legitimate spacer, operating or working for a business that requires a pilot's license.

I have had the second chip since I was eighteen years old. I've been using it more and more these last few years, since I discovered a wrecked Dignity Vessel that I thought I could mine for gold.

Instead, that ship mined me.

Now I take tourists to established wrecks all over this sector. I coordinate the trip, collect the money and hire the divers who'll make those tourists believe they're doing real wreck-diving.

Tourists never do real wreck diving. It's too dangerous. The process gets its name from the dangers: in olden days, wreck diving was called space diving to differentiate it from the planet-side practice of diving into the oceans.

We don't face water here—we don't have its weight or its unusual properties, particularly at huge depths. We have other elements to concern us: No gravity, no oxygen, extreme cold.

Those risks exist no matter what kind of wrecks we dive. So I minimize everything else: I make sure the wrecks are known, mapped, and harmless.

I haven't lost any tourists. But I have lost friends to real wreck diving. And several times, I've almost lost myself.

I haven't been wreck diving since the Dignity Vessel. I've turned down other wreck divers who heard I wasn't going out on my own any more and wanted me to supervise their dives.

What those divers don't understand is that I was supervising the Dignity Vessel when I lost two divers and destroyed three friendships.

I can't stomach doing that again.

So mostly, I camp at Longbow station. I bought a berth here, something I vowed I'd never do, but I don't spend a lot of time in it. Instead, I sit in the old spacer's bar and listen to the stories. Sometimes I make up a few of my own.

When I need money, I take tourists to established wrecks. Theoretically, those dives make everyone happy—the tourists because they've had a "real" experience;

the divers because they got to practice their skills; and me, because I made an obscene amount of money for very little work.

But obscene amounts of money don't do it for me. I bought the berth here so that I don't have to crawl back to my ship if I drink too much or feel like taking a half-hour nap. I haven't spent money on much else.

I used to use the money to finance my real passion—finding wrecks. I wasn't so much interested in salvage, although I'd been known to sell minor items.

I was interested in the history, in discovering a ship, in figuring out how it ended up where it was and why it got abandoned and what happened to its crew.

Over the years, I'd solved a few historical mysteries and found even more. I liked the not-knowing. I liked the discovery. I liked the exploration for exploration's sake.

And I loved the danger.

I miss that.

But every time I think on trying it again, I see the faces of the crew I lost: not just Jypé and Junior, who died horribly on that last trip, but Ahmed and Moïse and Egyed and Dita and Pnina and Ioni. All of them died diving.

All of them died diving with me.

I used to lull myself to sleep making up alternate scenarios, scenarios in which my friends lived.

I don't do that any more.

I don't do much any more. Except sit in the old spacer's bar on Longbow and wait for tourists to contact me for a job. Then I plan the visit, go to the wreck, plant some souvenirs, come back, pick up the tourists and give them the thrill of their lives.

With no danger, no risk.

No excitement.

The opposite of what I used to do.

2

SHE'S LAND-BORN. I DON'T NEED TO SEE HER THICK body with its heavy bones to know that. Her walk says it all.

The space-born have a grace—a lightness—to everything they do. Not all are thin-boned and fragile. Some have parents who think ahead, who raise them half in Earth Normal and half in zero-G. The bones develop, but that grace—that lightness—it develops too.

This woman has a heaviness, a way of putting one foot in front of the other as if she expects the floor to take her weight. I used to walk like that. I spent my first fifteen years mostly planet-bound in real gravity.

We have the same build, she and I—that thickness which comes from strong bones, the fully formed female body that comes from the good nutrition usually found planetside.

I used to fight both of those things until I realized they gave me an advantage spacers usually don't have.

I don't break.

Grab a spacer wrong and her arms snap.

Grab me wrong, and I'll bruise.

She sits down, says my name as if she's entitled to, and then raises her eyebrows as if they and not the tone of her voice provide the question mark.

"How'd you get in here?" I pull my drink across the scarred plastic table and lean my chair against the wall. Balancing chairs feels like that second after the gravity gets shut off but hasn't yet vanished—a half and half feeling of being both weighted and weightless.

"I have an invitation," she says and holds up the cheap St. Christopher's medal that houses this week's guest chip. Station management shifts the chip housing every week or two so the chips can't be scalped or manufactured. After five guest chips are given out, management changes housing. There is no predictable time nor is there predictable housing.

"I didn't invite you," I say, picking up my drink and balancing its edge on my flat stomach. I can't quite get the balance right and I catch the drink before it spills.

"I know," the woman says, "but I came to see you."

"If you want to hire my ship to do some wreck diving, go through channels. Send a message, my system'll scan your background, and if you pass, you can see any one of a dozen wrecks that're open to amateurs."

"I'm not interested in diving," the woman says.

"Then you have no reason to talk to me." I take a drink. The liquid, which is a fake but tasty honey-and-butter ale, has warmed during the long afternoon. The warmth brings out the ale's flavor, which is why I nurse it—or at least why I say I nurse it. I don't like to get drunk—I hate the loss of control—but I like drinking and I like to sit in this dark, private, enclosed bar and watch people whom I know won't give me any guff.

"But I do have a reason to talk to you." She leans toward me. She has pale green eyes surrounded by dark lashes. The eyes make her seem even more exotic than her land-born walk does. "You see, I hear you're the best—"

My snort interrupts her. "There is no best. There's a half a dozen companies that'll take you touring wrecks—and that's without diving. All of us are certified. All of us are bonded and licensed and all of us guarantee the best touring experience in this sector. It just varies in degree—do you want the illusion of danger or do you want a little bit of history with your deep space adventure? I don't know who sent you in here—"

She starts to answer, but I raise a finger, stopping her.

"—and I don't care. I do want you to contact someone else for a tour. This is my private time, and I hate having it interrupted."

"I'm sorry," she says and the apology sounds sincere.

I expect her to get up, leave the bar or maybe move to another table, but she does neither.

Instead she leans closer and lowers her voice.

"I'm not a tourist," she says. "I have a mission and I'm told you're the only one who can help me."

In the two years since the Dignity Vessel, no one has tried this old con on me. In the twenty years before, I'd get one or two of these approaches a year, mostly from rivals wanting coordinates to the wrecks I refused to salvage.

I've always believed that certain wrecks have historical value only when they're intact—not a popular belief among salvagers and scavengers and most wreck divers—but one that I've adhered to since I started in this business at the ripe old age of eighteen.

I point to Karl, a slight but muscular diver who has the best reputation on Longbow. He's not very good at finding things, but he has his moments. He was with me on that last run and we haven't spoken since we docked.

"Karl's good," I say. "In fact, if you want real adventure, not the touristy kind, he's the best. He'll take you to deep space, no questions asked."

"I want you," the woman says.

I sigh. Maybe she does. Maybe she's been led astray by some old-timer. Maybe she thinks I still have some valuable coordinates locked in my ship.

I don't. I dumped pretty much everything the day I decided I would only do tourist runs.

"Please," she says. "Just let me tell you what's going on."

I sigh. She's not going to leave without telling me. Unless I force her. And I'm not going to force her because it would take too much effort.

I take another swig of my ale.

She folds her hands together, but not before I see that her fingers are shaking.

"I'm Riya Trekov, the daughter of Commander Ewing Trekov. Have you heard of him?"

I shake my head. I haven't heard of most people. Among the living, I only care about divers, pilots, and scavengers. Among the dead, I know only the ones whose wrecks would have once made my diving worthwhile. I also knew the ones who had piloted the wrecks I found, as well as the people who sent them, and the politicians, leaders or famous people of their time, their place, their past.

But modern commanders, people whose name I should recognize? I am always at a loss.

"He was the supreme commander in the Colonnade Wars."

Her voice is soft, and it needs to be. The Colonnade Wars aren't popular out here. Most of the spacers sitting in this bar are the children or grandchildren of the losers.

"That was a hundred years ago," I say.

"So you do know the wars." Her shoulders rise up and down in a small sigh. She apparently expected to tell me about them.

"You're awfully young to be the daughter of a supreme commander from those days." I purposely don't say the wars' name. It's better not to rile up the other patrons.

She nods. "I'm a post-loss baby."

It takes me a minute to understand her. At first I thought she meant post-loss of the Colonnade Wars, but then I realize that anyone titled supreme commander in that war had been on the winning side. So she meant loss of something else.

"He's missing?" I ask before I can stop myself.

"He has been for my entire life," she says.

"Was he missing before you were born?"

She takes a deep breath, as if she's considering whether or not she should tell me. Her caution peaks my curiosity. For the first time, I'm interested in what she's saying.

"For fifty years," she says quietly.

"Fifty *standard* years?" I ask.

She nods. If I'm guessing her age right, and if she's not lying, then her father went missing before the peace treaties were signed.

"Was he missing in action?" I ask.

She shakes her head.

"A prisoner of war?" Our side—well, the side that populates this part of space, which is only mine by default—didn't give the prisoners back even though that was one of the terms of the treaty.

"That's what we thought," she says.

The "we" is new. I wonder if it means she and her family or she and someone else.

"But?" I ask.

"But I put detectives on the trail years ago, and there's no evidence he was ever captured. No evidence that he met with anyone from the other side," she says with surprising diplomacy. "No evidence that his ship was captured. No evidence that he vanished during the last conflicts of the war, like the official biographies say."

"No real evidence?" I ask. "Or just no evidence that can be found after all this time?"

"No real evidence," she says. "We've looked in the official records and the unofficial ones. I've interviewed some of his crew."

"From the missing vessel," I say.

"That's just it," she says. "His ship isn't missing."

So I frown. She has no reason to approach me. Even in my old capacity, I didn't search for missing humans. I searched for famous ships.

"Then I don't understand," I say.

"We know where he is," she says. "I want to hire you to get him back."

"I don't find people," I say mostly because I don't want to tell her that he's probably not still alive.

No human lives more than 120 years without enhancements. No human who has spent a lot of time in space can survive an implantation of those enhancements.

"I'm not asking you to," she says. "I'm hoping you'll recover him."

"Recover?" She's got my full attention now. "Where is he?"

The tip of her tongue touches her top lip. She's nervous. It's clear she isn't sure she should tell me, even though she wants to hire me.

Finally, she says, "He's in the Room of Lost Souls."

***

Ask anyone and they'll tell you. The Room of Lost Souls is a myth.

I've only heard it talked about in whispers. An abandoned space station, far from here, far from anything. Most crews avoid it. Those that do stay do so only in an emergency, and even then they don't go deep inside.

Because people who go into the room at the center of the station, what would be, in modern space stations, the control room but which clearly isn't, those people never come out.

Sometimes you can see them, floating around the station or pounding at the windows, crying for help.

Their companions always mount rescue attempts, always lose one or two more people before giving up, and hoping—praying—that what they're seeing isn't real.

Then they make repairs or do whatever it is they needed to do when they arrive, and fly off, filled with guilt, filled with remorse, filled with sadness, happy to be the ones who survived.

I've heard that story, told in whispers, since I got to Longbow Station decades ago, and I've never commented. I've never even rolled my eyes or shaken my head.

I understand the need for superstition.

Sometimes its rituals and talismans give us a necessary illusion of safety.

And sometimes it protects us from places that are truly dangerous.

***

"WHY IN THE KNOWN UNIVERSE WOULD I GO THERE to help you?" I ask, with a little too much edge in my voice.

She studies me. I think I have surprised her. She expected me to tell her that the Room of Lost Souls is a myth, that someone had lied to her, that she is staking her quest on something that has never existed.

"You know it, then." She doesn't sound surprised. Somehow she knows that I've been there. Somehow she knows that I am one of the only people to come out of the Room alive.

I don't answer her question. Instead, I drain my ale and stand. I'm sad to leave the old spacer's bar this early in the day, but I'm going to.

I'm going to leave and walk around the station until I find another bar as grimy as this one.

Then I'm going to go inside and I am, most likely, going to get drunk.

"You should help me," she says softly, "because I know what the Room is."

I start to get up, but she grabs my arm.

"And I know," she says, "how to get people out."

3

How to get people out.

The words echo in my head as I walk out of the bar. I stop in that barren corridor and place one hand against the wall, afraid I'm going to be sick.

Voices swirl in my head and I will them away.

Then I take a deep breath and continue on, heading into the less habitable parts of the station, the parts slated for renovation or closure.

I want to be by myself.

I need to.

And I don't want to return to my berth, which suddenly seems too small, or my ship, which suddenly seems too risky.

Instead I walk across ruined floors and through half-gutted walls, past closed businesses and graffiti-covered doorways. It's colder down here—life support is on, but at the minimum provided by regulation—and I almost feel like I'm heading into a wreck, the way I used to head into a wreck when I was a beginner, without thought and without care.

I don't remember much. I remember thinking it looked pretty. Colored lights—pale blues and reds and yellows—extended as far as the eye could see. They twinkled. Around them, only blackness.

My mother held my hand. Her grip was tight through the double layer of our spacesuit gloves. She muttered how beautiful the lights were.

Before the voices started.

Before they built, piling one on top of the other, until—it seemed—we got crushed by the weight.

I don't remember getting out.

I remember my father, cradling me, trying to stop my shaking. I remember him giving orders to someone else to steer the damn ship, get us out of this godforsaken place.

I remember my mother's eyes through her headpiece, reflecting the multi-colored lights, as if she had swallowed a sea of stars.

And I remember her voice, blending with the others, like a soprano joining tenors in the middle of a cantata—a surprise, and yet completely expected.

For years, I heard her voice—strong at first and unusual in its power— then blending, and mixing, until I can't pick it out any longer.

I didn't know if that voice—mixing with other voices—was an aural hallucination, a dream, or a reality. Sometimes I thought it both.

But it sneaks up on me at the most unexpected moments, sometimes beginning with just a hum. The hum sends shivers down my back, and I do whatever I can to silence the voices.

Which is usually nothing.

Nothing except wait.

***

After three days, Riya Trekov finds me.

I'm having dinner in Longbow's most exclusive restaurant. The food is exquisite—fresh meat from nearby ports, vegetables grown on the station itself, sauces prepared by the best chef in the sector. There's fresh bread and creamy desserts and real fruit, a rarity no matter what space port you dock on.

The view is exquisite as well—windows everywhere except the floor. If you look up, you see the rest of the station towering above you, lights in some of the guest rooms, decoration in some of the berths. If you look out one set of side windows, you see the docks with the myriad of ships—from tiny single-ships to armored yachts to passenger liners.

Another group of windows show the gardens with their own airlocks and bays, the grow lights sending soft rays across the entire middle of the station.

On this night, I'm having squid in dark chocolate sauce. The squid isn't what Earthers think of as squid, but an ocean-faring creature from one of the nearby planets. It has a salty nutlike taste that the chocolate accents.

I try to focus on the food as Riya sits down. She's carrying a plate and a full glass of wine.

Clearly she had been eating somewhere else in the restaurant, on one of the layers I can't see from my favorite table. But she had seen me come in and somehow, she thinks that gives her permission to join me.

"Have you thought about it?" she asks, as if she made an offer and I said I would consider it.

I can lie and say I hadn't thought about any of it. I can be blunt and say that I want nothing to do with the Room of Lost Souls.

Or I can be truthful and say that her words have played through my head for the last three days. Tempting me. Frightening me.

Intriguing me.

At odd moments, I find myself wondering how I would see the place, after all my years of wreck diving, after all the times I've risked my life, after all the hazards I've survived.

"You have," she says with something like triumph.

I continue to eat, but I'm no longer savoring the taste. I almost push my plate away—it's a crime not to taste this squid—but I don't.

I don't want her to see any emotion from me at all.

"But you have questions," she says as if I'm actually taking part in this conversation. "You want to know how I found you."

The hell of it is that I do want to know that. Hardly anyone knows I survived the Room of Lost Souls. I can't say that no one knows because the crew on my father's ship knew. And I have no idea what happened to all of them.

"I have people who can find almost anything," she says.

People. She has people. Which means she's rich.

"If you have people," I say with an emphasis on that phrase, "then have them go to the Room themselves and have them 'recover' your father."

Her cheeks flush. She looks away, but only for a minute. Then she takes a deep breath, as if she needs courage to dive back into this conversation.

"They don't believe that anyone can get out. They think that's as much a myth as the Room itself."

I don't know how I got out. My memory is fluid and try as I might to recover that moment, I can't.

When it becomes clear that I am not going to confirm or deny what happened to me, she says, "Your father is still alive."

I jolt. I had no idea the old man had made it this long.

"Have you ever asked him about the Room?"

I haven't, mostly because I never had the chance. But I don't tell her that. Instead, I say, "You spoke to my father."

She nods. "He's happy to know you're still alive."

I'm not sure I'm happy to know that he is. I prefer to think of myself as a person without a family, a woman without a past.

"Quite honestly," she says, "he's the one who recommended you for this job. I first approached him, and he says he's too old."

I slide my plate to the edge of the table to hide my face as I do the calculations. He turns seventy this year which is not old at all.

"He also said you have all the skills I need for this job." She hasn't touched her food. "He says he doesn't."

That much is true. He's never gone diving—at least that I know of. He captained a ship, but in the old-fashioned way—not as a hands-on pilot, but as a planetbound owner, who told others what to do.

We were on some kind of pleasure cruise, I think, when my mother and I wandered into the Room. Or maybe we were moving from one system to another.

I honestly don't know. I don't remember and I never asked him.

He wasn't around much anyway. After Mother vanished into that Room, he dumped me with my maternal grandparents and went in search of the very thing Riya claims she found: a way to recover people from the Room of Lost Souls.

"It makes no sense that he has refused to help you," I say as a bus tray arrives, sends out a small metal arm that sweeps my plate into its interior, and then floats away. "He's always wanted a way into the Room."

"He says the problem is not the way in, but the way out." She finally picks up her fork and picks at her now-cold food.

A chill runs through me. Does my father speak with that kind of authority because he has sent people in after my mother? Or because he's thinking of what happened to us all those years ago?

"And yet you claim you have that way out."

A serving tray appears with an ice cream glass filled with red and black berries separated by layers of cream. My coffee steams beside it. My standing order. I shouldn't take it, but I do.

"I do have a way out," she says.

"But you can't find anyone stupid enough to test it," I say.

She lets out a small laugh. "Is that what you think? You think I need a test subject?"

I take a sip of my coffee. It's slightly bitter, like all coffee on Longbow station. Somehow the beans grown here lack the richness I'd found on other stations.

"The way out has been tested. Going in and returning is no longer an issue. What I need is someone with enough acumen to bring out my father."

Something in her tone reaches me. It's a hint of frustration, a bit of anger.

Her people have failed her. Which is why she's coming to me.

"You've done this before," I say.

She nods. "Six times. Everyone survived. Everyone is healthy. There are no residual problems."

"Except they can't find your father."

"Oh," she says. "They have found him. They just can't recover him."

Now I am intrigued. "Why not?"

"Because," she says, "they can't convince him to leave."

***

I TAKE A BITE OF THE BERRIES AND CREAM. I NEED A few moments to think about this. I still feel as if she's conning me, but I'm not sure how. Or why she would do so.

"Why did he leave?" I ask.

She blinks at me in surprise. She clearly didn't expect curiosity from me.

"Leave?"

"You said he didn't show up for the treaty signings. That he essentially missed the end of the war. Why?"

She frowns just enough so that I realize she's never considered this question. She's been looking at her father as someone—some*thing*—she lost, not as a person in his own right. Oh, he has history, but it's history without her, and therefore not relevant.

"No one knows," she says.

Someone always knows. And if that someone is no longer alive, the answer would probably be in the records. Something this modern is easy to trace; it's the old stuff, like the Dignity Vessels, whose history gets lost to time that are difficult to figure out.

She's finally hooked me and she probably doesn't even know how. I don't want to return to the Room for my mother—I barely remember her and what I do remember is vague. I don't even want to return to face my own past.

I want to solve this mystery she has unwittingly presented me with. I want to know why a famous man, a man who won some of the most important battles of an important war, disappears before the war ends, and winds up in a place he knew better than to approach.

For the first time in years, the historian in me, the *diver* in me senses a challenge. Not like the old challenges, the ones that cost me so many friends and colleagues.

But a new challenge, one that will threaten me alone.

One that has the risk I miss combined with the historical mysteries that I love.

I try not to let my sudden enthusiasm show. I ask, as coldly as I can, "What are you paying?"

Her eyes light up. She seems surprised. Maybe she thought she'd never catch me. Maybe I am her last hope.

She names a figure. It's astoundingly high.

Still, I say, "Triple it and I'll consider the job."

"If you can get him out," she says, her voice breathless with excitement, "I'll give you one hundred times that much."

Now I'm feeling breathless. That's more money than I've earned in two decades.

But I don't have a use for the money I have. I can't imagine what I'd do with a sum that large.

Still, I negotiate because that too is in my blood. "I want it all up front."

"Half," she says. "And half when you recover him."

That's fair. Half would provide me a berth at Longbow and all of my expenses for the rest of my life. I'd never have to touch the rest of my money, the stuff I earned these past few years.

"Half up front," I say, agreeing, "and half when I recover him—only if you pay all expenses for the entire investigation and journey."

"Investigation?" She frowns, as if she doesn't like the word.

I nod. "Before I go after him, I need to know who he is."

"I told you—"

"I need to know *him*, not his reputation."

Her frown grows. "Why?"

"Because," I say, "in all the hundreds of theories about that Room, only one addresses the souls trapped inside."

"So?"

"So haven't you wondered how a man like your father got lost in there?"

I can tell from her expression that she hasn't considered that at all.

"Or why the name of the place—in all known languages—is the Room of Lost Souls. Are the souls lost because they entered? Or were they lost before they opened the door?"

She shifts slightly in her chair. She doesn't like what I'm saying.

"You've thought of this before," she says.

"Of course I have." I keep my voice down.

She nods. "You think he was lost before he went in?"

"I have no idea," I say, "but I plan to find out."

4

By the time I arrive at my berth, the money is in my accounts. That surprises me. I thought, after our conversation, that Riya would back out. She doesn't want to know her father as a human being. She wants only the image of him that she built up through her lonely childhood. The war hero who vanished. The strong man who got trapped.

Not a sad survivor who might have gotten lost long before he opened a door into a forbidden place.

Still, she has paid me and she has given me free reign.

I sit at the built-in desk and move the money to all of my accounts. I'm going to have to create some new ones before I leave so that my holdings are diversified. Before I do that, I pay for this berth for the next five years.

I warned Riya that the recovery could take a long time. She wants it done right. After I heard her tales of the previous attempts, I knew that part of the problem was she hired thieves and ruffians and risk-takers who specialized in cross-system possession recovery.

She hired disposable people who usually committed snatch-and-grabs. People who didn't care much for her mission or their own lives.

People who wouldn't be missed.

In that, they were a lot like me.

Riya and I finished the negotiations as I drank my coffee. She showed me the device her people had used to get out of the Room. I examined it. It looked unusual enough.

But she wouldn't give me its specs until I was ready to go to the Room.

I was fine with that. It gave both of us an illusion of control—me, the ability to say I was done before I went into the Room; and her, the belief that I had no idea how to use what she had shown me.

We made a verbal record of our negotiations. Both of our attorneys would work together to make a formal agreement which we would sign within the month.

She seemed nervous and uncertain, while I was nervous and happy. If someone had asked me before we started the negotiations who would feel what, I would have said that I'd be the uncertain one while she would be happy with all that we've done.

I fully expected her to terminate before I arrived in my berth.

Instead she paid me.

I finish transferring the money. I contact and pay my attorney, notifying her of her obligations in drafting this agreement.

Then I lean back in my chair.

For the first time since I've come to Longbow Station, balancing my chair on two legs does not satisfy me. The berth—with its built-in desk, view of the grow pods, and slide-out soft bed—no longer feels like home.

I need to move. I need to get out of here.

I need to spend the night on my ship.

***

By modern standards, *Nobody's Business* is a small ship, but by mine, it's huge. The *Business* can fly with a single pilot, but it's designed for twenty to fifty people.

When I was wreck-diving, I'd fly with ten or less and to me, that felt crowded. I'd close off the lower levels and lock up the cargo bays.

Sometimes I forget all the space I'm not using. The main level has the bridge and auxiliary controls. It also has the lounge, where I've put most of my viewing technology so that I can review dives. There are six cabins on this level as well, including mine.

The captain's cabin is two levels up. I never use it. My cabin is the same size as all the others. It looks the same as well except for the hard-wired terminal that I use when I don't want anyone hacking into my work.

Most (but not all) of the other systems on the *Business* are networked, and I'm up-front with any crew that I hire that I watch the systems diligently. If they put something on the system from a virus to a piece of information, it's mine. I've learned a lot that way.

The *Business* is docked in the permanent section of the station. I pay extra to keep her systems disconnected from the station's systems. I also bribe the officials to keep an eye on her, to make sure no one enters illegally.

Even so, I still run several security programs—all of them redundant. No one, not even the best hacker, can shut off all of them and still have time to case my ship.

So as I enter the *Business*, I stand in the airlock and check the first layer of security, seeing who—if anyone—has crossed this threshold since I last went through.

According to the programs, no one has.

I let myself in, breathing the stale air. I keep the environmental systems on low when I'm station bound—no sense wasting the energy. I power up, check more redundant security systems, and run a full diagnostic which I network to my own internal computer.

Long ago, I set up the *Business* and my single ship to communicate with me—mostly to make sure I remain awake and alert when I'm piloting either ship. But I also use the links to communicate with the *Business* about internal matters, mostly so that I'm not tied to the bridge.

The air has become cool as the environmental systems kick in. My cabin still smells faintly of incense from an abortive and mistaken attempt at relaxation on the last trip full of tourists. I make a mental note to have this room cleaned top to bottom, and then I sit at the hardwired terminal.

It's covered with a faint layer of dust. I haven't touched it in more than a year. I'm not even sure it'll power up.

But it does. Then it runs its own diagnostics and shows me all the security video from the cabin itself. I let the video play in a corner of the touchscreen while I access my financials.

I move ninety percent of the money that Riya paid me from my public accounts to my private ones. In a day or so, I'd create some new accounts, and divide the money up even more.

Then I settle into my chair and order lunch from my personal store.

I'm going to be here for a while. I have a lot of research to do and I don't want it traced.

***

I START WITH THE COLONNADE WARS.

I learned long ago to research everything, especially something you're certain of, because the memory plays tricks. And something you're certain of is most likely to be the thing you'll get wrong.

The Colonnade Wars lasted nearly one hundred years. The wars began as a series of skirmishes on the far end of this sector. Then actual war broke out toward the other end, on a small planet that had been colonized so long that some believed the humans on that planet actually evolved there.

Other battles—with different participants—started throughout the sector. At first, the weapons brokers and the mercenaries seemed to be the only ones who knew about the various skirmishes, but then it became clear that powerbrokers from several nation states were financing their favorites in each conflict. And sometimes those powerbrokers backed both factions at the same time.

The battle turned away from the petty internal squabbles—over land, over entitlements, over religious shrines—and turned against those who funded the fights.

Suddenly the powerful found themselves fighting on several fronts. Their massive armies and huge weapon systems were no match to the smaller, more creative warfare of their enemies.

And it looked, for a long time, as if the massive armies would break.

Enter Commander Ewing Trekov and his cohorts. All of them had been injured on one front or another. Most of them had come within a heartbeat of dying.

They ended up at the same treatment facility in the very center of the sector, and there they realized they had the same philosophy about the wars.

First, they believed that the Colonnade Wars were not wars at all, but a single war—a large, scattered battlefield that spread across several systems. These men and women, brilliant all, realized that fighting each front as if it were a separate war was what was destroying the army. A military could have no coherent strategy when it believed it was fighting a dozen wars at once.

So these people, as they healed, began studying the history of warfare—not just in this sector, but throughout human history, as far back as they could go. They discussed superweapons and super troops. They discussed a unified front and a robotized military. They explored remote fighting versus hands-on.

And they realized that nothing—no discovery, no miracle weapon, no well-equipped soldier—had ever taken the place of living commanders with a broad and unified vision.

And sometimes that vision was as simple as this: *Annihilate the enemy wherever you find him; whoever he might be.*

According to the histories, the man who first articulated that simple vision in the Colonnade Wars was Commander Ewing Trekov. Whether or not that's true is another matter.

What is true—and verifiable—is that Commander Trekov was the most effective leader of the war. He destroyed more enemy strongholds, captured more ships, and killed more soldiers—from all sides—than any other commander in the war.

He was supposed to be at the victory celebration. More importantly, he was supposed to be at the treaty signing ceremony. There wasn't just one treaty to be signed, but dozens—all with various governments (or, as one observer more accurately called them, various survivors). Trekov's presence wasn't just symbolic. He had negotiated several of the treaties himself.

Slowly I realize that I could spend the rest of my life reading about the Colonnade Wars and not get to all the details.

But those details don't concern me. All that concerns me is Commander Trekov.

And he's there but not there. Mentioned but not quoted. Observed but not really seen.

So I look up Trekov himself—when he was born, where he went to school, where he got his training. I look for family information—both on his family of origin and on the family he left behind.

I find Riya Trekov. She's significantly younger than I thought—born to Trekov's childless fifth wife nearly two decades after his disappearance. The other children want nothing to do with Riya —they believe her to be illegitimate, even though her DNA, her provenance (so to speak), is probably surer than theirs.

She has an easily accessible history—with degrees in accounting and business, a long career in high finance, and a personal wealth that's almost legendary. She accumulated those funds on her own, and is known around the sector as one of the most intuitive investors around.

Now she's invested in me—the first whim I could find in her entire history—and I wonder if this investment will pay off.

It's certainly turning into a research nightmare on my end.

Because the back-story on Ewing Trekov is confusing. His origins seemed lost in time. His education is classified as is most of his military experience. His battles are well documented, but that's about all of his life that's well documented

In the official histories, Trekov's personal history is deliberately vague. Which makes me wonder what's hidden there, and why no one is supposed to know.

For a while, I pace around the main level, trying to figure out how to discover the man and not the myth. And then I realize I'm researching him wrong.

I need to approach him as if he were a ship, a wreck I'm trying to discover.

I need to go backwards—from the last known sighting—and then I need to dig in the unofficial records, the half-hidden reports, and the highlights of his personal past.

Within forty-eight hours, my ship is stocked, my meager belongings on board, and I am heading to a little-known military outpost at what once was the edge of the sector.

The last recorded place anyone saw Ewing Trekov alive.

5

By all rights, this little outpost should be famous. It is not only the last place Ewing Trekov was seen alive, but it is also the place that he and the other commanders planned their strategy.

Military outposts are security minded. They make places like Longbow Station seem lawless. So I've come with letters of introduction from a general whom I supervised on tourist dives, a colonel who has known me since I began my career, and a government official who testified to the fact that my research is never for public purposes, only to find important "historical information."

I also have a letter of explanation from Riya Trekov, giving me permission to look into her family's confidential files. I have no idea if such a letter will open doors for me—I have never researched a human subject before—but I figure such a letter can't hurt.

This outpost is top of the line. The materials in the public areas are new and smell faintly of recently assembled metal. The lighting set higher than any I'd seen in a commercial outpost and the environmental systems are running at maximum comfort.

My tax dollars keep these soldiers in relative luxury, at least for space-farers. Most off-duty personnel walk around in shirt-sleeves and thin pants. Anyone on Longbow wearing such flimsy clothing would freeze.

I am given a bracelet which opens doors to the sections of the outpost that I'm allowed in. I've been given a guest suite—they don't call civilian quarters berths here—and with the suite comes the suggestion that I use it instead of staying shipside.

The suite is larger than the captain's cabins on most luxury yachts. It doesn't take me long to find out that I'm in one of the VIP rooms, courtesy, it seems to my ties with the general. His letter, which I scan after I look at my quarters, asks that the military treat me like one of their own.

Apparently they take that to mean they should treat me like they would treat him.

My rooms—and I have five of them—all have a view of the concentric rings, as well as a private kitchen (along with a personal chef should I not want cafeteria food), a valet should I require it, and a daily cleaning service. I don't require a valet or room cleaning service (although I know they won't waive that entirely), and I stress to everyone that I can how much I value my privacy.

My in-room computer system can access the public library of the base, and I start there, sitting on one of the most comfortable chairs I've ever used in my life, and scrolling through list upon list of recorded information pertaining to Commander Trekov himself.

It takes me nearly three days, but I finally find visual and audio files of his arrival on the base. No holographic files, at least not yet. But the visual and audio ones are the first I've found of the Commander at all.

He's imposing, nearly six-seven, which is tall for someone who spent his life in ships. His walk marks him as planet-raised as well, as do his thick bones and well-defined muscles.

He's not a handsome man, although he might have been once. His face is carelined and his eyes are sad. His hair is cut short—regulation then as now—and he has a fastidiousness that seems extreme even in this military environment.

I freeze one of the images of his face and frame it. Then I set it, as a holopicture, on the tabletop near my work station. I used to do this with ships that I was searching for. Ships that had disappeared or whose wrecks existed somewhere in a grid that no one had bothered searching for decades.

The images of the ships were always of them new. I used to compare that image with the wreck when I found it, not to find my way around it but so that I could get a sense of what hopes were lost in the ship's ultimate destruction.

But the image I keep of Ewing Trekov isn't of his youth, but of what he looked like toward the end. It's an acknowledgement that I'm searching for the part of him that's left over, the skeleton, the frame, the bits and pieces that survived.

I am no closer to getting him out of that Room by staring at his image than I got close to a wreck by staring at the original image of a ship. But I feel closer. I feel like this image holds something important, something I'm missing.

Or maybe, something I'm not yet allowed to see.

***

THERE ARE ACTUALLY PEOPLE ON THE OUTPOST WHO remember Ewing Trekov. They're old now, but most of them still work in their respective departments.

All of them were willing to talk with me and after days of interviews, only one seems to have a story that I can't find in the records.

Her name is Nola Batinet. She wants to meet in the officers' mess.

The mess isn't a dining hall, like the mess for regular soldiers. The officers' mess is divided into six different restaurants, each with its own entrance off the central bar. People in uniform fill that bar. They all have an air of authority.

A tiny woman stands near a real potted plant. The plant is taller than I am, probably taller than Trekov was. It's bright green, has broad leaves, and smells strongly of mint.

The woman is so small she could hide among the leaves.

As I approach, she holds out a small hand, which I take gently in greeting. The bones are as fragile as I feared. I'm careful not to squeeze at all, afraid I'll break her.

"We have a reservation in Number Four," she says.

Apparently the six restaurants here have no names. They go by number.

Number Four is dark and smells of garlic. There are no tables, just built-in booths with backs so high you can't see the other diners.

A serving unit—a simple holographic menu with audio capabilities—whisks us to the nearest booth. At first, I figure that the unit does so with each customer. Then I realize it's addressing Nola Batinet by name and has reassured her that they never let her favorite booth go when there's the possibility that she will come into the mess.

She thanks it as if it were human, nods when it asks if she wants the usual, and then she turns to me. I haven't even looked over the menu yet, but I'm not really here for the food. I take whatever it is she's having, order some coffee and some water, and wait until the server unit floats away.

"So," she says, "Ewing Trekov. I knew him well.

A faint smile crosses her face as she thinks of him. Her memories—at least the one she's lost in—are clearly pleasant.

A tray floats over with our beverages and with a large plate of cheeses and meats. I've never seen so many different kinds. The meats are clearly manufactured and are composed of so many different colors that I'm hesitant at first.

But Nola has been eating here for decades and seems no worse for it. After she eats a few pieces, I try one. The meat is peppery and filled with the garlic that I've been smelling. It's remarkably good.

"You're working for his daughter, right?" Nola asks. "The created one."

"She wants me to recover her father," I say, even though I've told Nola this when I first contacted her through the outpost networks. "She thinks he's in the Room of Lost Souls."

Nola nods just enough to confuse me. That tiny movement could mean she knows he's in the Room or that she has heard of this daughter's whim before. Or it could simply be an acknowledgement of what I have to say.

"Why does she want him?" Nola asks. "She never knew him."

And I had neglected to ask that question. Or maybe it wasn't neglect at all. If I knew, I wouldn't have taken the job, and the job had—in the end—intrigued me.

"It's not my concern," I say. "I'm just supposed to find him."

"You won't find him," Nola says. "He's long gone."

"How did you know him?" I ask, trying to get the conversation away from my job and back to her.

That small smile has returned. "The way most women knew him."

"You were lovers."

She nods. For a moment, her gaze rests somewhere to the left of me, and I know she's not seeing me or the booth or any part of Number Four. She's lost in the past with Ewing Trekov.

"You make it sound like he had a lot of lovers," I say.

Her eyes focus and move toward me. When they rest on me, they hold a bit of contempt. She knows what I'm doing, and she doesn't like it. She wants to control this conversation.

"A lot of lovers," she says, "a lot of wives, and more children than he could keep track of."

Maybe that's where the disapproval comes from. Riya Trekov isn't special in Nola's eyes.

"He didn't care about family?" I ask.

Nola shrugs. "The man I knew didn't have time for relationships. Not long ones, any way. His entire life was about the wars and the entire sector. He saw lives the way we see stars—something far away and yet precious. Individual lives meant something to him only for a few weeks. Then he moved on."

There's pain in her voice.

"He moved on from you," I say as I take some yellow cheese. It's slimy against my fingers, but I don't dare put it back.

"Of course he did. Anyone who believed he would do otherwise was a fool."

But the bitter twist on the word "fool" makes it clear to me who "anyone" was.

"You said that you know things no one else does." I make myself eat the slimy cheese. It's remarkably good. Rich and sharp, a taste that goes well with the pepper and garlic of the meat.

"Of course I do," she says. "And some of it will go with me to my own death."

It's my turn to nod. I understand that kind of privacy.

She sets the plate near the edge of the table. Something moving so fast that I can barely see it whisks the plate away.

"But the story I'm going to tell you," she says, "isn't one of those. And it's not something you'll find in the histories either."

I wait.

"It's about his plans," she says with that secret smile. "He never planned to go to any of the ceremonies and he wasn't going to sign any treaties."

"He told you this?" I ask, mostly because she's surprised me. Everything I've seen says he fully intended to go to the ceremonies. He sent notice as to when his ship would arrive. He had a contingent of honor guards waiting for him on another outpost nearer to the ceremony. He even had a dress uniform ordered special for the occasion.

"No, he didn't tell me anything," she says. "At least, not in so many words. He wasn't that kind of man. I figured it out, years later."

***

SHE FIGURED IT OUT WHEN SHE REMEMBERED WHAT happened that last day. How he'd been, how sad he seemed.

They met in his VIP cabin. It was large and lovely with a bed the size of her quarters. But he wasn't interested in sex, although they had some.

He ordered food for them—an astonishing meal for a place this remote. Yet he didn't enjoy the meal. He picked at it, letting much of it go to waste. She couldn't—she hadn't had a meal this good since she was stationed here.

But he waited until she was finished before he spoke.

"How do you do it?" he asked. "How do you save lives when you know they'll just go to waste?"

She didn't understand what he meant. "Go to waste?"

"Most of your patients here, they'll get sent back out and they'll die out there. Or they'll go home and they won't be the same. Their families will no longer know them. Their lives will be different."

"But not wasted," she said.

He kept picking at the food. He wouldn't look at her. "How do you know?"

"How do you?" she asked.

He shrugged.

"Most of these soldiers I see, they're children," she said. "They'll go home and remake their lives."

He shrugged again. "What about career military?"

She set her own fork down and pushed her plate away. She realized then she had to pay attention to this conversation, that it seemed to be about one thing and was really about another.

"Are you worried about what'll happen to you after the ceremonies?" she asked.

He shook his head, but he still didn't look up. He was developing a bald spot near his crown, and he hadn't paid for enhancements. The small circle of skin made him seem vulnerable in a way she'd never noticed before.

"This isn't about me," he said, but she didn't believe him.

"You can stay in the military," she said. "They need planners. Even in peacetime, they'll need a standing army. Governments always do."

"Seriously, Nola," he said with some irritation. "It's not about me."

"What is it about then?" she asked.

He shook his head again. The movement was small, almost involuntary, as if he were speaking to himself instead of her.

"Your units? The people under your command?"

He kept shaking his head.

"Your injured?"

"The dead," he said softly.

She was silent for a long time, hoping he would elaborate. But he didn't. So she struggled to understand.

"We can't help them," she said. "Even now with the technology that we have, the knowledge that we have, we can't help them. We just try to prevent death."

"And how do you do that?" he asked, raising his head. "How do you know who's worthy?"

She frowned. She was a doctor. She had been all her adult life. "I don't choose the worthy ones. That's not my decision."

"I've seen triage," he said. "You pick. You always pick."

Her breath caught.

"I don't choose by worthiness," she said softly. "I choose by my skill level. I choose by time. Who will survive the intervention? Who will take the least amount of time so that I can get to other injured? Who will be the least amount of work."

That last made her face flush. She'd never admitted it to someone else before—at least not to someone who wasn't a doctor, someone who wasn't really faced with those decisions.

"That's how you pick who's worthy," he said.

His words made her flush deepen.

"Doesn't that bother you? Don't you look at the ones you didn't even try to save, the ones you sacrificed for the others, and wonder about them? Don't you sometimes think you made the wrong choice?"

Her face was so warm now that it actually hurt.

"No." She wanted to say that with confidence, but her voice was small, smaller than she'd ever heard it around him. "If I thought I always made the wrong choice, I couldn't do my job."

"But in the wee hours, when you're alone...?"

She was staring at him. He hadn't looked up once.

After a moment, he shook his head a third time, as if he were arguing with himself.

"Never mind," he said. "I'm just tired."

Which gave her an excuse to leave.

She had no sense it was the last time she'd see him. The next day, he had left the outpost.

And she never heard from him again.

***

"I'M SORRY," I SAY AFTER GIVING HER A MOMENT TO return from the memory. "I don't see how all of that meant he didn't plan to go to the ceremony. I don't see how this relates to the Room of the Lost Souls."

She raises her eyebrows in surprise. I get the distinct feeling she has just decided I'm dumb.

"He wasn't thinking about the future," she says. "He was thinking about the past."

"I got that," I say, and hope the words weren't too defensive. "But he makes no mention of the ceremonies or of the Room. So I'm not sure how you made the connection all these years later."

A slight frown creases the bridge of her nose. "The Room," she says, "is a pilgrimage. Some say it's a sacred place. Others believe only the damned can visit it."

My breath catches. I haven't heard any of that before. Or maybe I have. I used to make it a practice of not listening to stories about the Room because I believed no one could understand that place if they hadn't been there.

"All right," I say, "let's assume he knew that. How do you know he went there next?"

"His crew says so." She crosses her arms.

"I know that," I say. "But you found this interchange important. Enlighten me. Why?"

"Because I was stupid," she snaps. "He wasn't talking about me. He was talking about himself. *His* choices. *His* way of doing things. *His* losses. I'm sure he was reflecting on them because everyone expected him to celebrate the end of the Wars."

"He should have celebrated," I say.

She smiles faintly, then nods. For a moment she looks away. I can see her make a decision. She takes a deep breath and uncrosses her arms.

"I agreed with you back then. I figured he should have been at his happiest. But he wasn't so wrong about our jobs. I spent a lot of years as the chief surgeon on a military ship, and mostly I handled minor injuries and not-so-serious illness. But when we were in the middle of a battle, and the wounded kept pouring in, I just reacted."

I nod, not wanting her to stop.

"I worked my ass off," she says. "And people died."

She leans back, and rests her wrist on the side of the table. "I never, ever counted how many people I saved. I still don't. I suppose I can look it up. But I know to the person how many have died under my watch," she says softly. "I'll wager Ewing knew too. And each one of those deaths, they take something from you."

A little piece of yourself, I almost add. But I don't want her to think I'm sympathizing falsely, and I'm not willing to reveal as much of myself to her as she has revealed of herself to me.

"He wouldn't have been talking about death if he was going to go to those ceremonies," she says. "He wouldn't have been looking at the past. He would have been looking toward the future, at what we could build."

She sounds so confident. Yet they were just lovers, in passing, on a military output. How well did she really know him, after all?

And how can I ask her that without insulting her further?

So I try a different tack, partly to take my mind off those irritating questions and partly because I want to know.

"You said it's a pilgrimage. You said only the damned can get in."

Her frown grows. "Have you never heard of the Room?"

"I know it," I say, choosing my words carefully. "I just don't know the legends."

And I should. I used to believe that the legends were more important than "facts" or histories or stories they could verify. Because legends held a bit of truth.

"Do the damned go to get cleansed?" I ask.

Her mouth closes. She takes a breath, sighs, then gives me that faint smile all over again.

"Some say the Room bestows forgiveness on those who deserve it." That faraway look appears in her eyes.

"And those who don't?" I ask.

Tears well. She doesn't brush at them, doesn't even seem to notice them.

"They never come back," she says. Then she frowns at me. "You think he went for forgiveness, not to disappear."

I shrug. "The timing works. If he completed his pilgrimage to the Room, he could have gone to the treaty-signing ceremonies."

"With a pure heart," she whispers.

"He was a hero," I say without a trace of irony. "Didn't he have one already?"

And for the first time, she has no answer for me.

***

SHE HAS LED ME IN A WHOLE NEW DIRECTION. I'M NOT looking for the remains of a man. I'm looking for something unusual, something special.

A man has a history and occasionally he becomes a legend. But a man is rarely special by himself. Sometimes he becomes special in a special time. Sometimes he rises beyond his upbringing to become something new. Sometimes he starts a movement, or alters the course of a country.

And sometimes—rarely—he changes an entire sector.

Like Ewing Trekov supposedly did with his friends as they developed a plan for the war.

But that story implies that he didn't work alone. That if he had died before he came to this outpost, someone else would have picked up that mantle. That someone might not have performed as well. He—or she—might have done better. There's no way to know.

But like all humans, Trekov wasn't entirely unique.

The Room of Lost Souls is unique.

No one knows exactly what it is or how it got to be. No one knows where it started or who built it or why.

Places develop myths, become legends in ways more powerful than any human being ever can. Because beneath each legendary human is the reminder that he *is* human, that what makes him special is how he rose above his humanness to become a little bit more than the rest of us.

Not a lot more. Just a little bit.

Trekov was a man who had more children than he could count, who made love to women but apparently didn't love them. A man who cared more about his work than his family.

A man like so many others.

A man who just happened to be the right man for the war he found himself in.

But the Room—the Room existed before humans settled this sector. The Room shows up in the earliest documents from the earliest space travelers.

And because it's so old, and because no one knows exactly how it works or why it's here or how it came to be, myths grew up around it.

People go on a pilgrimage.

Smart people, like Ewing Trekov.

People believe the Room will do something for them. Change something about them. Satisfy something within them.

The legends around the Room are fraught with danger. Space travelers are warned to stay away from it. I remember that much.

I *heard* that much.

But I'm not sure when. Or where. Or from whom.

Still, I need to heed my own advice.

I need to research the thing I think I know the best.

I need to talk to the one other person who remembers it vividly.

I have to talk to my own father.

Much as I don't want to.

6

My father lives halfway across the sector, on a small planet whose only inhabited continent counts itself as one of the losers in the Colonnade Wars.

He's lived there for nearly two decades—and it's a sign of how out of touch we are that I actually had to look that information up.

My father's house is a maze of glass, stairs, and steel. From the outside it seems haphazard, rooms on top of rooms, but from the inside, it has a wide-open feel, like the best cruise liners, designed not to take you to a destination but to help you enjoy the journey.

He built his house in the center of a large blue lake, so at night the water reflected the skies above. If those skies are clear, it seems like he is in space, traveling from one port to another.

He doesn't seem surprised to see me. If anything, he's a little relieved.

I arrive in the middle of the afternoon and he insists I stay there. I nearly decline until he shows me the guest room. It is at the very top of the house, glass on all sides except the part of the floor that covers the room below. The bed seems to free-float between the blueness of the lake and the blueness of the sky.

The sun—too close to this planet for my tastes—sends light through the glass, but environmental controls keep the room cool and comfortable. My father shows me where those controls are so I can lessen the gravity if I want.

It takes me a while to realize that my father's house is modeled on the station that houses the Room of Lost Souls. We meet in the center room—the room that would be the Room of Lost Souls if we were on that station—and he offers me a meal.

I decline. I'm too nervous in his presence to eat anything.

My father is no longer the man I remember, the man who cradled me when I got out of that Room. That man had been in his late thirties, tall and strong and powerful. He'd loved his wife and his daughter, making us the center of his life.

He'd commanded ships, built an empire of wealth, and still had time for us.

He abandoned everything to figure out how to get my mother out of that place. His businesses, his friends.

Me.

Which makes it so strange to see him now, essentially idle, in this place of openness and reflected light.

He still looks strong, but he hasn't bothered with enhancements. His face has lines—sadness lines that turn down his eyes, and pinch the corners of his mouth. He has let his hair go completely white, along with his eyebrows, which have become bushy. His mustache—something I considered as much a part of him as his hands—is long gone.

He makes our greeting awkward by trying to hug me. I won't let him.

He acts like he still has affection for me. He does make it clear that he has followed my career—as much as he can through what little I make public.

But he has respected my wishes—the wishes I screamed at him the last time I ran away from my grandparents—and has stayed out of my life.

"You sent Riya Trekov to me," I say.

I can't sit in the chair he's offered me. I'm too restless in his presence, so I pace in the large room. The glass here opens onto the other rooms. Through their glass walls I can see still more rooms, and at the very end, the lake. Looking at it through all this glass makes it seem far away, and not real. It looks like a holograph of a lake, the kind you'd see on the distance ships of my childhood.

"I figured if anyone could help her, you could." His voice is the same, deep and warm and just a little nasal.

I shake my head. "You're the one who has done all the research on the Room."

"But you're the one who has dived the most dangerous wrecks ever found."

I turn toward him then. He sits in the very center of the room. His chair is made of frosted glass and the cushions that protect his skin are a matching white. He looks like he has risen from the floor—a creature of glass and sunlight.

"You think this is like a wreck?" I ask. "Wrecks are known. They're filled with space and emptiness. They have corners and edges and debris, but they're part of this universe."

"You think the Room isn't?" He folds his hands and rests his chin on his knuckles.

"I don't know what it is. You're the one who has spent his life studying the damn thing."

So much for trying to hide my bitterness toward his choices.

He grimaces, but nods, an acknowledgement that my bitterness has its reasons.

"Yes," he says. "I've studied it. I've traveled to it countless times. I've sent people in there. I've repeated the same experiments that have been tried since it was discovered. None of them work."

"So why do you think Riya Trekov's device will work?" I ask.

"Because I was with her on one of the missions," he says. "I watched people she paid go in and come back out."

"Empty-handed," I say.

He nods.

"Yet she thinks someone can bring her father out."

"She might be right," he says.

"And if he can come out, so can Mother."

"Yes." The word is soft. He lifts his chin off his folded hands. The knuckles have turned white.

"If you believe this and you think I'm the one who can bring a lost soul out, how come you didn't ask me to do this yourself?"

"I did," he says. "You turned me down."

I snort and sink into one of the nearby chairs. He's right; he did contact me. I had forgotten it among his many summonses, all of which I ignored. But this one had been his last, a long plea explaining that he not only had a way into the Room of Lost Souls, he had a way to survive it.

"You used to say you never wanted me to go back in there. You discouraged me from even going near the place, remember?"

I had been fifteen and full of myself. I'd run away from my grandparents half a dozen times. They were in constant mourning for my mother, and believed I was no substitute. It was pretty clear that they blamed me for her loss.

The final time, my father came after me, and I told him I could get my mother. I was the only one who'd come out alive. He owed me the chance to try.

He had refused.

I left him—and my grandparents—and never contacted any of them again. Although he kept trying to reach me. And I kept glancing at, then refusing, his messages.

"I couldn't risk it," he says. "We barely got you out that first time."

"Yet you recommended me to go in when Riya Trekov comes to call. Because she has a way out or because you don't care any more?"

His cheeks flush. "You didn't have to agree."

The chair is softer than I expect. I relax into it. "I know," I say, giving him that much. "Her plea interested me."

"Because of your diving," he says.

I shake my head. *Because I have nothing left.* But I don't say that.

"I recommended you because you're trained now," he says. "Of everyone I know, you have a chance, not just to get out. But to get out with something. You've become an amazing woman."

I no longer know him. I can't tell if he's being sincere or if he's trying to convince me.

He's still a man obsessed. I wonder what he'll do if he recovers the remnants of Mother. Her "soul" or her memory or even her self. He's lived for decades without her. If she's still alive, she's spent double her initial lifespan inside a single Room.

I came here to find out one thing. So rather than debate the merits of my experience or the point of his obsession, I say, "Tell me what happened. How did we end up at the Room? How did we lose Mother?"

"You don't remember?" he asks.

The lights, the voices. I remember. Just not in any detail.

"My memories are a child's memories," I say. "I want the real story. The adult story. Mistakes and all."

7

We had no home. I didn't remember that, just like I didn't remember moving onto the ship six months before. My parents had sold our house and had put everything they had into his business, a fleet of cargo ships that ran all over the sector.

The business had become a success when my father stopped caring about the ethics of the cargo he carried. Sometimes he brought food or agricultural supplies to far-flung outposts. Sometimes he brought weapons to splinter groups rebelling against various governments.

He didn't care, so long as he got his payment.

He made so much money, he no longer needed to run the fleet, but he did. Still, my mother begged him to buy land and he did that too. This land, kilometers and kilometers of it, the entire lake and the surrounding greenery.

He promised her they would retire here.

But they were still young, and he loved travel. He commanded the lead vessel because he owned it, not because he was good at piloting or even at leadership.

He tells me about the trips, about the deliveries, about the crew. The ship had a contingent of forty regular with two dozen others whom he hired for larger jobs. Sometimes they worked the cargo, sometimes they repaired the ship. Always they listened to him, whether he was right or not.

But he wasn't the one who commanded them to the Room of Lost Souls. That was my mother. She had heard about it, studied it, thought about it.

She wanted to see it.

She didn't believe a place that old—human-made—could exist in this part of space.

"She was trying to be a tourist," he says now. "Trying to make all this travel work."

But I wonder. Just like I wondered about Trekov. If my mother had done all the studying, had she been planning a pilgrimage? Because of my father's business or because of some problem all her own?

I realize, as I'm sitting there, I know even less about her than I know about my father. I only know what I remember, what her parents told me in their grief, and what my father is telling me now.

"I took her there," he says. "With no thought, no study. I thought it just an ancient relic, a place that we could see in half a day and be gone."

"Half a day," I mutter.

He looks at me, clearly startled that I spoke.

"So she planned to go to the Room?"

"That was the point of our visit," he says.

"And she wanted to take me?" I can't believe anyone who studied that place would bring a child to it.

"You suited up and followed her. You grabbed her hand as she went through that door. I think you were trying to keep her from going inside."

But I wasn't. I was entranced with the lights, as fascinated as she had been.

"I saw you go in," he says. "I called to you both, but the door closed behind you."

"And then?" I ask.

"And then I couldn't get you out."

Minutes became hours. Hours became a day. He tried everything short of going in himself. He smashed at the window, tried to dismantle the walls, sent in some kind of grappler to grab us. Nothing worked.

"Then, one day, the door opened." His voice still holds a kind of awe. "And there you stood, your hands over your ears. I grabbed you and pulled you out, and held you, and the door closed again. Before I could go in. Before I could reach inside..."

His voice trails off, but I remember this part. I remember him clinging to me, his hands so firm that they bruise me. It feels like he holds me for days.

"You couldn't tell us anything," he says. "You didn't think any time had gone by at all. You were tired and cranky and overwhelmed. And you never wanted to go in again."

"You asked?"

He shakes his head. "You said. Without prompting. We stayed for a month. We never got her out."

And then he ordered the ship to leave. Because he knew he could spend the rest of his life struggling against that place. And he had a child. A miracle child, who had escaped.

"I dropped you with your grandparents and came back. I figured I could go in and get her. But I couldn't. Except for you, I didn't know anyone who had gotten out."

"Which is why you want me to go," I say.

He shakes his head. "I've found people willing to go inside. Nothing comes out."

"I thought you said you went with Riya Trekov. That she has a way out."

"She does. People go in. They come out. But they're always alone."

Now I ask him. "What'll you do if you get her? She won't be the same. *You're* certainly not."

"I know," he says, and for a moment, I think he's going to leave it at that. Then he adds, "None of us are."

***

WE TALK LONG INTO THE NIGHT.

Or rather, I listen as he talks.

He tells me what he knows about the Room. He has an almost encyclopedic knowledge of the place, combined with a series of theories, myths, and legends he has collected over the decades.

What it all comes to is what I already know: No one knows who built the Room or the station it's on. No one knows when it was built—only that it predates the known human colonization of this sector. No one knows what its purpose was or why it was abandoned.

No one knows anything, except that people who go in do not come out.

Unless they're protected by Riya Trekov's device.

The device, as my father explains it, is a personal shield, developed by a company that's related to my father's old business. The shield relies on technology so old that few people understand it.

Sometimes I think all of human history is about the technology we've lost. We're constantly reinventing things.

Or recovering them.

Apparently, this device is something reinvented.

How it works is simple: It acts like a spacesuit—creating a bubble around the user that contains both environment and gravity and anything else the user might need.

It has the same flaws a spacesuit has as well: It allows a person to enter an environment but not interact with it—or at least, not interact in important ways.

But the shield is different from a spacesuit as well. From the first discovery of the Room, humans have tried to enter wearing spacesuits, and that has not worked.

So Riya Trekov's device negates something—or protects against something—that a spacesuit does not. Somehow, that device—that bubble it creates—is the perfect protection against the Room.

At least that is what my father would have me believe.

That's what Riya Trekov showed me briefly on Longbow Station.

But now I have more qualms than before. Because the more my father talks, the more disgusted I become.

He has spent all this time studying the Room. He has made that Room his life's work.

Yet he has never been able to risk that life, not even to pull me or my mother out of the Room.

As he paces around me, I think of all the times I've gone into a wreck, how I've looked for trapped divers, what I've risked to recover their bodies.

I've only failed to recover one.

On the Dignity Vessel. I left one of my divers behind because he was trapped in something I did not understand.

Like I do not understand Riya Trekov's device.

Like I do not understand the Room.

People have devoted their lives to the mystery that is the Room, and have learned nothing.

Unlike them, I do not want to learn anything. I don't even want to recover my mother or Ewing Trekov—both of whom I consider dead.

I want to see the Room for myself, to satisfy some curiosity that has plagued me since I was ten years old. In that, perhaps, I am more like my mother than my father. If his story is to be believed—and I am not sure it is—then my mother just wanted to see the anomaly for herself.

Which is, in part, what I want to do. But more than that, I want to see, experience, and understand from an adult perspective what had so influenced me as a child.

I want to know how much the Room formed me, the embittered wreck diver, the woman who once believed that preserving the past was more important than any money that can be made from it.

The woman who believed—and maybe still does—that the past holds secrets, secrets which, if understood, can teach us more about ourselves than any science can.

I do not tell my father any of this. I let him believe I'm doing a job. I pretend to be interested in all that he tells me.

And I pretend to be surprised when he tells me he wants to join me.

He says he wants to see the Room one last time.

8

It takes months to put a team together. The people who want to go to the Room are not experienced divers or experienced space travelers for that matter. The people who do not want to go are the ones I need.

I am able to buy some of them—money goes a long way with people who live on the edge—but I cannot buy all. Most importantly, I cannot buy Karl, who was with me on the Dignity Vessel job.

At first, he won't even talk to me. But eventually, his curiosity gets the better of him. He agrees to meet me in the old spacer's bar in Longbow Station.

I am at the station alone. I told my father that I would not be able to recruit when he was around. He has a reputation for being difficult and for thinking he's in charge. I actually got him to sign legal documents attesting to the fact that he would not run anything on board my ship or do anything to command (or jeopardize) my expedition.

I am using three factors in picking my team: I want people who are creative—both mechanically and intellectually;

I want people who have dived the most dangerous wrecks in the sector; and I want people who are honest.

Finding the last two is relatively easy—divers have to be honest or they don't survive. The survivors are usually the ones who have been on the most dangerous missions.

But most divers leave the creativity to the person in charge of the mission. Since, in the past, that was me, I never had the opportunity to work with other dive team leaders.

Except Karl.

He started his business after I quit mine. He took over my routes, and I didn't interfere with him because I believed I would never wreck dive again.

But that isn't the only reason I want him.

I want him because he's trustworthy—and he's dangerous.

I don't know a lot about his personal history, but I do know a few things, things I've observed and things he's told me.

He's ex-military and he's excellent with a knife. He can kill anything—and has, twice on dive trips, once before I knew him, and once after he opened his own business and trusted the wrong person.

He's cautious to a fault and yet oddly fearless. I say oddly because I've seen him back away from a dive because of worries about it, only to see him conquer those worries and go in.

I respect that about him.

I also know he can get my people back to Longbow if something happens to me.

He can get them back and he can handle my father.

Those elements are more important than creativity, more important than diving ability, more important than survival skills.

He has just come off a run of his own. He won't tell me where, which leads me to believe he has discovered a wreck he doesn't want me to know about.

His angular face seems even thinner than before, and his gray eyes seem silver in this light. He looks older, as if leading his own expeditions has taken something out of him.

He wears a thin white shirt over his slender chest. His pants are too loose, suggesting that the thinness in his face isn't my imagination. He's lost weight.

He straddles a chair across from me, using the chair's back as protection between us. He wraps his arms around it and stares at me.

"You have some nerve," he says.

"Yes, I do." I smile.

He doesn't smile back.

Then I sigh and let the smile fade. "I would like to hire you for a run."

"And I would like to tell you to go fuck yourself." But he doesn't move. "But if I do, you'll just keep asking me. So I came to hear what you have to say and to tell you no in person."

I understand why he's angry at me. I also understand if he never works with me again. When I hired him to go to the Dignity Vessel, I didn't tell him what we were diving, even though I knew.

I didn't tell any of my team. I didn't want them to bring preconceptions to the dive.

That was just the first mistake I made on that trip—if I had spoken up, we might not have gone in, and we wouldn't have lost two divers.

Karl swore he'd give up diving after that, but he didn't. It's a hard profession to renounce. There isn't much left in this sector that allows the kind of freedom, risk and adventure real wreck diving does.

"Just hear me out," I say to him.

This time, I tell him everything. I tell him about my past, about my father, about Riya Trekov and her father. I tell him about the Room and its dangers. I tell him about the pilgrimages and the quasi-religious symbolism others have found in the place.

Then I tell him what I remember of the Room itself.

That's when he finally moves. Just a little, but enough so that I know I've hooked him somehow.

And I'm not quite sure how.

"If what you say is true," he says, "this is the second wreck you want to bring me to that's out of time."

My breath catches. I knew that the station and the Room don't belong. I haven't allowed myself to make the mental comparison to the Dignity Vessel.

"You think it's related to the Dignity Vessel?" he asks.

"I don't know," I say. "There's always a chance. But I worry about preconceptions."

"Yeah," he says dryly. "I remember that about you."

The words sting.

"I might be wrong," I say. "Preconceptions might be necessary. I don't know. I just know I'm going to do this job as if it's a dive, and I want the best team possible."

"You realize the chances of someone dying on this trip are very high," he says.

"Yes." I swallow. That someone will probably be me.

He sighs. He's clearly thinking about the offer. We haven't talked money yet. I doubt money will mean much to him.

"What do you get out of this?" he asks. "Reconciliation with your father?"

I shake my head. "I want nothing from him."

"Yet you bring him along. That could compromise us right there."

I like the word "us." I didn't expect it. But I don't show him that I've noticed.

"I know it could," I say. "I'll need help minimizing contact with him."

"And your mother." He shakes his head. "This is fraught with emotion. You taught me that dives should have no emotion."

And yet our last dive was filled with it. We were trying to recover a body, and we couldn't. It devastated us both.

"I know," I say.

"If I go," he says, "I run the mission."

My entire body freezes. "How can it be my mission if you run it?"

"The dives," he says. "Anything to do with the Room. If I say we pull out, we pull out. If I say we leave someone behind, we leave them."

I bite my lower lip. I'm barely breathing.

"C'mon, Boss," he says, using my old divers' nickname. "You know that's why you're asking me to go. I'm the only one qualified, and the only one you'll listen to. You know that when I say we have to leave, I'll be right."

I let out the breath I was holding. Part of me has relaxed. He *is* right. That's why I chose to approach him. Because of our history. Because I know he's more cautious than I am, and because he has nothing at stake.

Except proving to me that I can be wrong.

"No grudges?" I ask.

He smiles for the first time. It's a sad smile. "I've lost two divers in the years since the Dignity Vessel. I don't know if I would have made the mistakes you made, but I've made some of my own. I think I'm finally beginning to understand you. So, no grudges. I'll do what's best for the mission, not what's best for Riya Trekov or your father. Or for you."

I nod. "You haven't even asked about money."

"I know you'll be fair," he says. Then his smile grows. "And I've always wanted to see the Room. The most mysterious place in this sector. I say let's go."

***

MAYBE THAT'S WHY SUCH PLACES CATCH AND KILL so many. Because they capture the imagination. Certainly that's why so many stories spring up around them.

And so many myths.

With Karl at my side, I do even more work. We sort through the repeated histories, and try to find the sources of various legends. We trace the Room in the modern era as best we can, and we ghoulishly make a list of all the souls known to have been lost in the place.

There are more than five hundred—and that's just recorded losses. Who knows how many others there were? No one has kept track of the abandoned single ships found near the station or people on a pilgrimage all on their own.

In passing, I say to Karl that what we've learned isn't worth the time we've spent. And he says what we've learned is that there are no odd recorded stories, things that don't quite fit into the other stories.

Maybe there's even a recognizable pattern. There certainly is to the losses. What happened to my father and his crew is the same as what happened to the very first ship that discovered the place, centuries ago.

"The same," I say, "except me coming out of that Room."

"Except that," Karl says.

***

In the end, we put together a team of ten, not counting me or Karl or Riya or my father.

Karl will lead the mission once we arrive at the station. Until then, I am in charge. I'll be in charge again when we leave the station as well. It's only when we're docked—when we're near the Room—that Karl will have control.

We use the *Business*. It has never been so full—at least not as long as I owned it. My father has the captain's cabin, which assuages my conscience. I've cut him off from all command and all control, which has to be difficult for him. So I reward him with the best quarters on the ship.

Riya has the third best cabin. Mine is second best, and with its dedicated hardwired computer, I don't want anyone near it.

The dive team has the rest of the main deck and Karl has the only room on the upper deck. It has the best views, and is impressive, should anyone visit him. I want him to look powerful and in charge, even before he is.

Some—including my father—believe that I placed Karl in charge of the mission at the station because Karl and I are lovers. The dive team knows differently—it's no secret in the diving community how angry Karl was with me after the events with the Dignity Vessel—but they're under orders not to correct that misperception.

Karl helped me vet the dive team. Two women who'd been on some of his previous dives, an old timer who has more experience than me and Karl combined, three superb and fearless pilots, three young men hired more for their strength than their diving ability, and another old colleague, a woman who had accompanied me on my earliest professional dives.

I have decided to treat this as a real dive, which means that we are focusing on the station, not just the Room. From everything that Karl and I have found, it seems people who have gone to the station have gone for the Room—or only spent time in the Room.

No one has given the habitats more than a cursory examination, not even the scholars. In fact, the scholars have mostly relied on the discovery of others, being too afraid to examine things themselves.

On the first day out, I brief the dive team about our mission. We meet in the lounge. The *Business*'s lounge is not for recreation. I put all of my playback and analysis equipment here. I also use it to analyze upcoming dives. There are comfortable chairs as well as two sofas, but they're arranged in an uncomfortable pattern—a semicircle facing the various screens and portholes.

Nine members of the dive team are here, as well as myself and Karl. I have banned Riya and my father from attending any meetings about the upcoming dives. The missing member of the team is the pilot who is currently flying the ship.

The team spreads around the lounge, trying to look casual, but I recognize the emotions here. Everyone is excited. The work is what they live for—it's what I used to live for—and when they're approaching something new, it's thrilling, not frightening.

I haven't felt the thrill yet. I haven't felt fear either, which I consider a victory. What I am feeling is nervous. I have no idea how any of this will play out.

I'm not sure how I want it too.

Still, I try to maintain an upbeat attitude, like I used to do when I started dangerous dive missions in the past. I walk in front of the screens, looking every member of the team in the eye as I speak.

I am not as honest with them as I was with Karl. I do mention problems—my father, the loss of my mother to the Room, which is why Karl will lead once we get to the station—but I do not mention my own reservations.

Instead, I talk about the history.

"We are not looking for items to resell," I say, although everyone probably knows that. After all, they've signed on to dive with me and Karl, not some salvage divers or treasure hunters. "We're looking for information—anything that will tell us about the station, about who built it, how it came to be here—why it's out here at all so far away from everything—and what its purpose actually is."

"Do we know if the Room is an integral part of the station?" asks Roderick. He's slight but broad-shouldered, a landbound pilot, who somehow became one of the most highly rated in the sector. I supervised his first shift with the *Business* and was impressed. He found my control shortcuts without explanation in a matter of minutes.

"We know nothing," I say. "We don't know if the Room's intentional or part of an accident."

"We do know," Karl says, "that the habitats next to the Room have been destroyed. But we don't know how. We don't know if someone destroyed them trying to block access to the Room or if the Room was something else and an accident or an explosion or something gone horribly wrong created the damage that we'll find around it."

"We're not scientists," says Odette. She's the oldest diver, whom I'd partnered with long ago. She is standing in the back of the lounge near the main exit, her stick-thin arms crossed. She looks delicate against the bulkhead, as if nothing could prevent her from floating off into space. "How are we supposed to know what happened in there or what any of it means?"

"Between us, we have centuries of experience with ancient technologies." I'm mostly talking to her and Karl now, but some of the other divers we hired have it as well. "We'll know as much or more than any scientist we bring out here."

"Besides," Karl says, "we are going to bring back as much information as we can about the station. Our goal is to be the definitive historical mission for the station and the Room."

"Is that why you wouldn't give us a timeline?" asks Tamaz, one of the young male divers we hired for his strength and not for his great experience. He has muscles along his arms and chest that I haven't seen in most divers. He probably had to have a special suit made.

But I wanted his strength in case we have to pull someone out of the Room. We've already established that machines can't do it, but a person might be able to. A very strong, very motivated person.

"We are not giving you a timeline because we can't," I say. "The Room's past history shows that people can sometimes be inside for hours or a day before coming out again."

Although the only history that showed that was mine. All of the people hired by Riya and my father came out within hours of going in, just like they were supposed to.

Both Karl and I felt the dive team didn't have to know this aspect of the Room's history—nor did they have to know the fact that I had already been inside. I did not want to be seen as an expert on the interior, particularly when I can't remember much about it.

"If there's no treasure inside, why would people go in?" asks Mikk, another of the strong young men. He's taller than Tamaz, but otherwise looks very much the same. I would have considered them brothers if I hadn't known otherwise.

"There's treasure," I say before Karl can comment. "But it's not the monetary kind. We warned you about that when we hired you for the dive."

Mikk waves his right hand. It's bigger than my thigh. "I'm not thinking for me. I mean all these five hundred people you say never came out. Why go in in the first place?"

"You're not religious, are you, Mikk?" Davida asks softly. She's one of Karl's hires, a regular wreck diver who has the standard lean physique along with skin so taut it looks stretched over her frame.

"So?" he sounds defensive.

"That's what a pilgrimage is, something religious." Davida sounds sure of herself, but she's obviously not that religious either.

"Pilgrimages have religious connotations, yes," Odette says from her post in the back. This time, the dive team looks at her as if they haven't really noticed her before. "But a pilgrimage is also a mission to a special place, not just a sacred place. One could say this is a pilgrimage."

Her gaze is on mine. She knows some of my family's history, but I don't believe she knows all of it.

"It certainly is for Riya Trekov," I say to cover my own discomfort. "She believes her father's soul is trapped in this place, and she believes we can recover it."

"Do you?" Tamaz asks me.

I think for a moment—the lights, the voices building one upon another, the clutch of my father's arms as he holds me tight.

"No," I say after a moment, "but that doesn't mean we aren't going to try."

9

THE STATION IS BIGGER THAN I REMEMBER, BIGGER THAN my father's descriptions of it, bigger than anything mentioned in the archives.

It looms ahead of the *Business* like a small asteroid or a tiny moon. It's gray in the constant twilight of space, the reflection of far away stars making it seem brighter than it actually is.

There are no visible lights on the station, nothing that marks it as a landing site or an outpost or some kind of way station. There are no energy readings, faint or otherwise.

I fly us toward the station as Roderick, Karl, and the other two pilots—Hurst and Bria—monitor the audio bands, trying to find any sign of life coming from the place.

The five of us sit shoulder to shoulder as we work the controls. The cockpit feels crowded, even though it's built for ten or more. The station shows up on my viewscreen and in my controls as well as in the portholes throughout the ship.

Out of deference to my father, we do not dock on the exterior docking ring. This was where his large cargo ship docked—it couldn't go any deeper into the station itself—and this was where the nightmares that have haunted the rest of his life began.

Instead, I pick a smaller ring on the upper level, where the habitats are still intact. From here, it looks as if we've approached a darkened but working space station. Reflections in the exterior windows of the station make it seem like someone is moving inside.

That startles Hurst—he even points it out—but Karl and I have approached so many wrecks, we're used to the phenomenon.

"It's just us," he says. "We're seeing our own reflections."

Still Hurst works the sensors. He's not convinced. He's already spooked, and I don't like that. I need solid, steady people, not superstitious ones given to outbursts.

I make a mental note to keep him away from the pilot's chair during this part of the mission. And I will tell Karl that later on.

Right now, we settle into work. First we have to use our own equipment to map the station. Then we'll proceed with a dive plan.

"It's bigger than I thought," Bria says. She has steady hands, which I appreciate, and a quick sense of humor. Her dark head is bent over the controls, her hands moving across them as if the *Business* is a ship she's spent her entire life aboard.

"It's a lot bigger," says Hurst. His hands are shaking. He made it clear to us when he was hired that he'd never flown a mission like this. He'd mostly done combat zones.

Active danger—shots, explosions—doesn't bother him. He's a quick thinker in that kind of situation, and since Karl and I didn't know what we were facing, we wanted one pilot with experience flying in and out of a constantly changing situation.

"All our previous readings are wrong," Karl says, and that's when I look. He gives me his handheld.

Previous specs showed the station to be one-quarter to one-half the size of this station.

"Are we in the right place?" Roderick asks.

I nod. The coordinates are right. The middle of the station is right as well.

But I don't trust it. I do my own scan.

The readings on the exterior of the station are correct except for the station's size. The strange metal, the age of the station itself, its unusual structure match the past specs.

"What the hell?" Roderick mutters.

Karl has frozen beside me. The hair on the back of my neck has risen.

"There are a million explanations," Bria says, oblivious to our reaction. "You said no one explored the whole thing. Maybe no one mapped it either. You're relying on stuff you've found in databases, which could be corrupted or tampered with or just plain wrong."

"True," Hurst says. "I've run into this all over the sector. Particularly in the lesser known parts. No one really cares how big something is unless they need to. Most people aren't that accurate."

But this is a place that ships have come to on pilgrimages. This is a place that has been studied.

And my own sense as we approached was that it has become bigger.

I swallow hard, but I don't say anything.

Instead, I get out of the pilot's chair and sweep my hand toward it, looking at Karl's angular face.

"It's your mission now," I say.

He hesitates. Then he takes a deep breath and slides into the pilot's chair. Of the five of us in the cockpit, he is, by far, the weakest pilot, but he knows what I'm doing.

I'm symbolically relinquishing command.

I have to.

I'm already not thinking rationally. I'm making things up based on my past experience.

And that terrifies me.

***

I LEAVE THEM TO MAPPING. I GO TO MY QUARTERS and log onto my dedicated computer. I call up files I haven't looked at in years.

Files that I stored after the Dignity Vessel.

Files on stealth technology.

Modern ships have stealth technology. It shields our ships from each other's instruments. But it does not make the ship completely invisible. It simply makes us invisible to all but the naked eye. If we pass in front of a porthole, someone on that ship will see us.

Our weak stealth technology is hard won. We've been working on it for generations, always seeking to improve it, and never doing so.

True stealth technology—the kind that actually makes a ship invisible (and, in some cases, impossible not just to see but to hear and touch)—is extremely dangerous. The kind of stealth that the ancients had actually changed the ship itself (or whatever the stealth was applied to). Some believe that the ship dissolved and reformed at a particular point. Others think it went out of phase with everything else in the universe. And still others believe that it actually leaves this dimension.

No one knows, exactly, because we have lost more technology than we have kept. The ancients had things we've never had. We didn't understand what they did or the way that they built things. We lost that knowledge somewhere along the way.

Our military—our scientists—have attempted to reverse engineer all kinds of things, including the kind of stealth the ancient Dignity Vessels had, but to no avail.

An old military diving buddy of mine once said that kind of stealth tech was banned, the knowledge deliberately lost. She claimed that hundreds would die every few generations or so when someone tries to revive the technology. She believes it is beyond our grasp.

It certainly was on the Dignity Vessel that Karl and I dove. The stealth tech there was based on interdimensional science. Those ships didn't vanish off radar because of a "cloak" but because they traveled, briefly, into another world—a parallel universe that's similar to our own.

When I first heard this theory, I recognized it. It's the one on which time travel is based, even though we've never discovered time travel, at least not in any useful way, and researchers all over the universe discourage experimentation in it. They prefer the other theory of time travel, the one that says time is not linear, that we only perceive it as linear, and to actually time travel would be to alter the human brain.

But my experience in that Dignity Vessel showed me that it's possible to open small windows in other dimensions. Only in practice those windows don't work the way they do in theory. They explode or get stuck or ships get lost.

People get lost.

Is that what we're facing here? Yet another version of ancient stealth tech?

My skin is crawling.

That would be too simple, and too much of a coincidence.

And it wouldn't explain the voices.

This is why I have given over the controls to Karl earlier than I planned. Although I'm beginning to doubt the wisdom of that. Karl is as familiar with ancient stealth-tech as I am and is scarred by it too.

I hope it won't affect his judgment here.

I stand and pace my small quarters, and as I do I remember the other reasons I hired Karl to run things.

Riya.

My father.

My mother.

Those voices.

No preconceptions, that's my motto. And I need to wait until mine are under control before I face the team all over again.

***

By the time I come out, the station is mapped. It is definitely larger than our research told us it would be. Karl wants to bring in my father, and I can't contradict him even though I don't want to use my father for anything.

We meet in the lounge. Fortunately, Karl has kept Riya out of this meeting. Most of the dive team is here and all of the pilots. The *Business*, safely docked, has its automatic alarms on in case something happens.

Still, this close to a dive, I hate leaving the cockpit unattended.

Karl reminds everyone that he is in charge now. Then he introduces my father—using all of his very impressive credentials—and says,

"I invited him into this meeting because he's been here before. He knows a lot about the station and even more about the Room."

Karl looks at me. My father is standing next to him, dwarfing Karl. My father, with his planet-bound height and muscle, looks almost superhuman compared to the divers. And even though he's older than everyone except, perhaps, Odette, he seems much more powerful.

I don't like the contrast.

"The changes in what we're expecting are enough to make me reassess the mission," Karl says.

I turn toward him, shocked. This isn't the man I hired all those years ago. This isn't Karl the Fearless.

He sees my look and holds up his hand to silence me. "I've learned over the years that it's best to talk about the unexpected, and even better to get the dive team's read on it. We're here to take extreme risks, but not *unnecessary* risks."

I dig my teeth into my lower lip, so that I don't contradict him—at least not yet. At least not this early in the very first meeting he's called.

Karl explains our findings, and he uses some impressive graphs and charts and diagrams that he's clearly worked on in the short time since he called the meeting. Then he turns to my father.

"What do you make of this?" Karl asks.

My father walks in front of the displays, his hands clasped behind his back like a professor grading a student's work. I get the sense that he likes the attention and is milking it.

"Your worry isn't necessary," he says after a minute. He addresses Karl like the rest of us aren't here. "I've seen this before."

I remain still in the back of the lounge. Odette crosses her arms. Karl tilts his head, obviously intrigued.

"Every time I come here, the station is bigger." My father does not pause, even though he should have. The sentence sends a ripple of interest through the group and would have given him the attention he obviously craves. "I think it's programmed to build new units, which is why the habitable ones are on the outer layers, not in the middle."

It's a plausible explanation, and no one asks him for his proof. I would have. My father is not a scientist, and he didn't back up what he just said with any statistics or experimentation. Just observation and a supposition.

"So it's normal," says Bria with something like relief.

"There's nothing normal about this place," my father says.

"How do we test the growing theory?" asks Jennifer. She's one of my hires, and she looks at me as she asks this, all wide eyes and innocence. But I've known her for a while, and Jennifer isn't innocent. She's annoyed that I've been forgotten, and she's pointing me out to the others on purpose.

I'm glad for the opening. "We test all theories. That's why it's best to go slow. The more we learn before we go to the Room, the better off we'll be."

"You actually think we'll learn something new about the Room?" Davida asks. She's sitting by Jennifer and Roderick on the couch. They glance at her in surprise.

"Why else come on this mission if you can't learn something new?" Roderick asks.

"It's just that this thing has existed for so long and no one knows anything about it," Davida says. "That's beginning to creep me out."

"We know some things," my father says and goes into his lecture on the history of the Room. He doesn't seem to notice that he's talking mostly about conjecture and theory, but some of the others do. They squirm. He's lost the attention he worked so hard to gain.

It takes Karl a while to shut my father down, but he finally does. Then Karl looks at me as if my father's lack of social graces are my fault.

I give Karl a half smile and a shrug.

Karl gets my father to sit. Then Karl sets up the dive roster for the following day—Bria piloting one of the four-man skips (so that our teams don't have to free dive to get into far sections of the station) and Davida, Jennifer, and Mikk in the upper habitats—with a promise of more when we meet that night.

The team shifts, but this time it isn't because of my father's long-windedness. It's because they're excited.

It's because they're ready.

We all are.

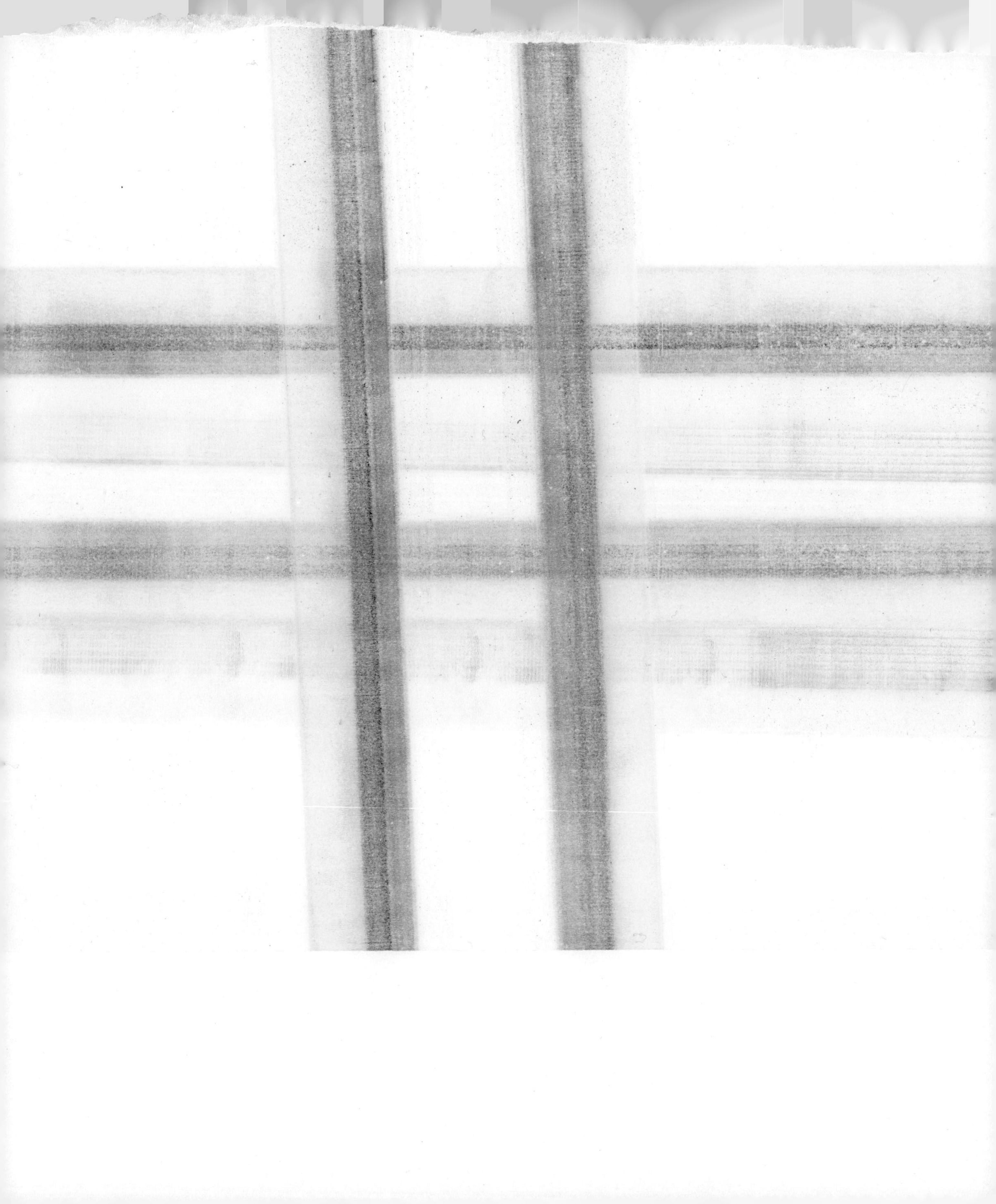

10

For the next three weeks, we dive the station, making detailed maps, exploring the new and old habitats, sharing small discoveries.

Every night we meet in the lounge and watch the captured imagery of that day's dives. The divers narrate and the others ask questions. That way, we all have the same information.

We learn quite a few things—the built-in furniture is the same in all of the habitats, although in the "new" section, as Karl likes to call it, it's not dented or warped or even scratched.

The new sections contain a few other things—remotes attached to entertainment equipment, equipment that doesn't seem to work "although it might if we can find a good way to power the entire station," my father says. "Maybe the entertainment programming is supposed to come from the damaged central area."

I don't like having my father in the lounge at night. He's not methodical and he's given to supposition. I think supposition is deadly. Karl finds it fascinating, but he can separate out the supposition from fact.

I'm not sure some of the younger divers can. Although they occasionally find my father long-winded, they seem to like him. They may even admire him.

I don't ask anyone what they think of him, not that they'd give me an honest opinion. Everyone is aware that he is my father and that we aren't on the best of terms.

Indeed, everyone else talks to him more than I do.

Including Riya, who daily complains that we are wasting her time and money. From the moment we arrived, she wanted us to go into the Room and do nothing else. Fortunately, Karl is in charge of this part of the mission, and Karl must talk to her, reminding her that caution is our byword, and even if we don't recover her father on this trip, the information we gather might make it possible to recover him on the next.

One night, she came to me to complain. I waved her off. "You gave me as much time as I needed," I reminded her.

"Yes," she said. "I gave *you* that, not him."

"And I placed him in charge while we're at the station. I trust him."

She glared at me. "I hope that trust isn't misplaced."

So far, it doesn't seem misplaced. I approve of the way he's handling the team—dividing assignments based on experience and on interest. It soon becomes clear who likes going through debris-crowded destroyed habitats, and who prefers a minute exploration of the pristine edges of the station.

He also has kept track of the pilots—who handles the skip best in tight quarters and who is the most observant. And he hasn't lost track of the Room.

Once a week, he and I have gone around its exterior. The first time, we mapped it. The second time, we mapped again to see if it had expanded. The third, we just observed.

The station hasn't grown while we're here. And we've seen nothing untoward about the Room, although on that first dive I was surprised to learn that the Room is encased on all sides.

For some reason, I thought part of it was open to space. I'm assuming that's because I saw the lights and they seemed to lead somewhere. And also, I'm sure I thought the Room had unlimited space because it has taken so many bodies.

When you peer through the main window, you can see none of those bodies. In fact, you can't even see the lights. It looks dark and empty, like the still-intact habitats.

Only when you shine a light inside, it disappears into the darkness. It does not reflect back at you.

My father claims to recognize all of this, which is making Karl grow more and more exasperated with him. At one point, in one of our nightly meetings, Karl snapped at him, "I asked you to tell us everything you knew about the Room."

My father shrugged. "I have."

"Yet each night, you have some new observation, some new memory."

My father didn't seem perturbed at Karl's tone. "You think small details are important, things I noticed, but never really thought much about. So when I remember them, I tell you."

Karl asked if there were other things like that which my father noted, things he wanted to tell us.

My father shrugged again. "I'm sure I'll remember when the time comes."

Karl looked at me and caught me rolling my eyes. But I said nothing to him or my father. Karl asked to command this part of the mission because he believed my observations and judgments would be compromised.

He's only beginning to realize that my father's are as well.

***

THE READINGS HAVE COME BACK FROM THE NEW habitats. They're composed of the same material as the rest of the station, only it isn't worn down by centuries. It does seem newer, just like the interior furniture does. A lot points to my father's theory—that the structure is being built new—but I am not sure how.

If the station is adding to itself over time, I'm not sure what materials it's using. My father seems ignorant of the law of matter conservation, so he thinks it possible to create something from nothing. I've never seen that happen.

Then, one night, I woke bolt upright on my bed, worried that the matter being used to make the new station comes from the bodies of the dead.

I had to do the calculations just to calm myself down. They showed me that even with every part of a body being used, there wasn't enough material.

Either the station had some kind of supply, something we didn't recognize, or it was bringing matter in from elsewhere.

Or it wasn't growing itself. It was revealing itself, like I feared.

And I found a lot of evidence to support that theory. At least, evidence that part of me wanted to believe.

When we left the Dignity Vessel, we left one of our divers—Junior—inside. Because we were worried that he might still be alive but in some kind of time dilation, Karl and I went back to see if we could rescue him. Failing that, we hoped to find a way to help him die.

We learned that, indeed, Junior had gone through a time dilation, but not the kind we thought. He had aged so rapidly that the upper half of his body, still in its dive suit had mummified.

His waist and legs had only been dead for a day but his upper half, his torso and his face had been dead for centuries.

I found myself wondering if the station wasn't going through the same sort of time split. Maybe the station was stuck in two different timeframes . Maybe it was stuck. And like some stuck objects, it was slowly sliding out of whatever held it.

Which would explain how it "grew" each time my father had visited, and why the newer areas didn't seem to age. Maybe the time split here was the opposite of the one we'd found on the Dignity Vessel.

Instead of time progressing rapidly in the part we couldn't reach, it was progressing slowly there—or maybe not at all. That the parts of the station being revealed were in a section between time, between dimensions.

I was no scientist, and I had no way to test my theories. I didn't even want to mention them to Karl. He had enough to worry about.

I did mention one worry, however. I told him it concerned me that the station expanded outward, and I made him promise no skip and no diver would travel to the outer edges.

I didn't want another Junior. I didn't want someone to get stuck between two times or two dimensions or two universes.

I wanted to be cautious and in this, as in everything else, Karl agreed.

***

EVERYTHING SEEMS TO BE GOING FINE, AND DESPITE MY discomfort, my mood has improved. The divers are enjoying their dives and no one has had a close call or been injured.

We're not lulled into a complacency, however. We know that the worst part of the dive is ahead, and that it belongs to me.

I've been preparing, and not just in my visits to the Room. I've spent most of my free time examining Riya's device. I've run it through my computers, trying to find its origin, and cannot.

It is made of familiar materials, but they're grafted onto a center that I do not recognize or understand. The materials in that center aren't anything like what I found on the Dignity Vessel or here at the station, and for that I'm relieved.

It doesn't seem to do much when it turns on—I get a small energy spike, and lights run along the edges of the device. But I don't sense the bubble or see momentary shimmer or something that would imply an actual shield going around me.

But a lot of things work without being obvious. And I'm not testing the device in zero-G. I'm testing in Earth Normal, in full environment. I don't want to test it outside the ship, lest I cause problems.

I wish I knew more about the device, but Riya can't tell me much. She says she got the shield through her father's connections.

She can tell me nothing else.

So I memorize the exterior dimensions of the Room, so that I can find the edges even if I can't see them. And I try to ignore the music in my head, which seems to grow each and every day.

Grow isn't exactly the right word. The music plays a little longer each time I "hear" it. It isn't louder or any more insistent. It's just harder to shut off.

I'm actually becoming used to it. In the past it would distract me and I would have to concentrate on anything outside myself while the voices sang. Now they're a background accompaniment, and I wonder if I would actually notice them if I weren't planning to go back inside the Room so soon.

The night before I go in, Karl calls me to his quarters. I haven't been up to them since I assigned them. I'm startled to see that he's blocked the view of the station, but has left the portals that open to the space views clear.

He's sitting near the clear portals, his back reflected in them. His eyes are wide, and for the first time since I've given him control, I worry that he's not up to it.

Something has unsettled him.

"You okay?" I ask as I sit across from him. My back is to the station. Although the portals are opaqued against it, I can feel it looming, almost as if it's a living entity, one that grows and changes and becomes something else.

"I'm a little uncomfortable," he says and shifts in his seat as if to prove the remark. "I've put this conversation off too long."

I stiffen. One of the risks of giving him control is that he would keep it, that he would make the mission—and in some ways, the ship—his. I trusted him not to do that, but that trust suddenly feels fragile.

"What's going on?" I ask, careful to keep my voice calm.

"I've been thinking a lot about tomorrow's dive," he says. "I don't think you should do it."

The words hang between us. I make myself breathe before responding.

"Have you seen something that makes the dive untenable?" I ask.

He shakes his head. “The dive is fine. I think we should go ahead with it. I just don’t think you should be the one to go in.”

My face heats. “That’s the whole point of this mission.”

“Going into the Room to recover Commander Trekov is the point of this mission—the central point, the one you and I agreed on. But this whole mission is larger than that, and we’re learning some great things. We wouldn’t have done that without you.”

He clearly planned that little speech. It sounds forced.

“Who’ll go in?” I ask.

“Me,” he says.

“Alone?” The word squeaks out. I’m surprised and can no longer hide it.

“I have the most dive experience next to you,” he says.

“Actually, that’s not true. Odette does.”

“All right, then,” he says. “You and I have the most diving experience on dangerous wrecks. She’s spent the last fifteen years on tourist runs.”

“Like me,” I say softly.

“You haven’t spent fifteen years at it, and if that were the only problem, I’d ignore it.”

I want to cross my arms and glare at him. But I don’t. I put him in charge for a reason. I’m going to hear him out.

“So what are the other problems?” I ask.

He takes a deep breath. “Your father for one.”

“I don’t like him,” I say. “We have history. So what?”

“You have a shared history. And it has to do with the loss of your mother.” Karl folds his hands across his knee, then unfolds them. He’s clearly nervous.

"We discussed this," I say. "That's why you're in charge."

"I know," he says. "But that loss is significant. It caused the rift between you two and it changed both of your lives. I've heard your story about the Room and you were entranced by that place."

"I was happy to get out," I say, repeating what my father told me.

"But you went in willingly. What if the Room causes some kind of hypnosis? What if you're still susceptible to it? It's irresponsible to send you in on the first dive."

I'm about to protest when I register the word "first."

"You think there will be more than one dive?" I ask.

"There has to be," he says. "We do it by the book. We map and observe and then we discuss. If we're going to remove something from the Room, we do so on the final dive."

"So you want to do at least four dives," I say.

He nods. "The problem is that we only have one device, so only one of us can go in at a time. You'll be looking for your mother. You know you will—"

I'm shaking my head, but deep down, I know he's right. Of course, I'll be looking for her. And for Commander Trekov, and the others trapped in that place.

"—and you won't be focused on the small but necessary details. I will. I've made a point of not looking at your mother's image or Commander Trekov's. Even if I see them, I won't recognize them. They'll be part of the entire package. I won't be tempted to move too quickly."

I swallow hard. "Why not send someone else in? It's a risky mission. You're in charge. You should stay out here."

"It is risky," he says. "But you'll be out here. And if I can't survive with that device, no one else will be able to either. So you'll abort and get everyone out of here."

"We can make that decision together," I say. "Send in another diver."

"Who? Odette? Mikk? Who are you going to send in, knowing that most people who have gone inside that Room have died? Are you willing to risk their lives?"

I don't say anything. We both know that I wasn't when I hired them. I knew there was only one device and I would be the one to use it. Everyone else was brought in, initially, to help extract me from the Room, not to go in and explore.

"I'm not willing to risk yours either," I say.

"You don't get a choice." He's calmer now. His gaze meets mine. Those gray eyes reflect the darkness of the portals behind me. "You put me in charge."

"But I still have the device," I say. "And I'm not giving it to you."

"No, you don't have it," he says. "That's why I wanted to meet you here. I had it removed from your quarters."

I feel so violated I have to prevent myself from lunging at him. No one goes in my cabin. No one even has access.

Except I gave him command. He has the codes.

He must have looked them up.

"I'm sorry," he says.

My face is so hot that it feels inflamed. I'm gripping my chair, and it takes all of my energy to stay in one place. Fighting him will do neither of us any good.

In handing over command, I also gave him implicit rights to imprison me in my own ship. I'm not going to give him the satisfaction.

"You know this is the right decision," he says.

I'm not going to acknowledge that.

"You're the one who taught me that emotion can be deadly to a dive," he says.

I get up. I trust myself to walk to his door and to get out. But that's all I trust.

Still, I stop. "You will never violate the sanctity of my cabin again."

He nods. "I'm sorry," he says again. "I had Odette wear her recorders and keep them on. She knows if she touched anything other than the device I'll have her hide."

It isn't the touching that bothers me. It's the entering.

That is my private space. No one else belongs in there.

My quarters are so private they almost feel like an extension of myself.

I don't say any more. I step into the hallway, wait until the door closes, and lean against the wall.

A part of my brain already acknowledges that his decision is sensible. I know that when I calm down, I'll agree. Four dives into the Room is actually the minimum for a dangerous area.

Not one, like I'd been planning.

I'd been thinking like a survivor of a disaster, not like a wreck diver.

And Karl understands that.

He's protecting me from myself, yes, but more than that, he's doing his job.

He's making sure the mission is a success.

And I hate him for it.

11

I INSIST ON BEING IN THE SKIP THE NEXT MORNING. Karl lets me on board, but he won't let me pilot. I am strictly an observer.

Today's pilot is Roderick. Karl's diving partner—a misnomer, really, since Karl has to go in alone—is Mikk. I've brought my suit just in case, but Karl gave it a filthy look as I entered the skip.

He doesn't want me entertaining any thoughts of diving the Room. I'm along for two reasons: as a courtesy to me, and so that we don't have to explain our plan to my father or Riya.

They've proven more rigid than I could ever be. As time has progressed, they've complained more and more about the habitat dives. They want someone in the Room and they want it soon.

They don't even know we're going in today. In the last several meetings, Karl has left out the diving rosters and locations until my father was gone.

Karl thought I would object to keeping them in the dark about the Room dive. But I don't. I haven't liked the access he's given them from the beginning. That's more than I would have offered.

Roderick is good at flying the skip in enclosed spaces. We want the skip as close to the entry point as possible. That way, the divers don't have to cover a lot of known ground before going into the important part of the dive. It saves time and could save lives if someone got into trouble.

In this case, the skip would have to go into the destroyed habitats. It's not as dangerous as it sounds. Most of the debris has been cleared by time or by scavengers. Roderick flies with the portals closed, which makes me feel blind.

But he focuses on instruments, and he's so good with them that I don't complain. Not that I have any right to, anyway.

Because the distance between the Room and the *Business* is so short, Karl has already put on his suit. It's an upgrade from the days when we dove together, but it resembles the one he had before.

Karl likes redundant systems. His suit is expensive and a little bulky. It has an internal environmental system, like all suits, but it also has an external one.

He used to carry only two extra breathers. Now he has four, and they're larger than the ones he used to have. Apparently the Dignity Vessel experience has had a greater impact on him than he's willing to admit.

Instead of a slew of weapons in the loops along his belt, he carries a few tools and his knife. The knife has a

long curved blade and has saved his life more than once.

I find myself staring at it throughout the short journey, wondering what he would use it on inside that Room.

Mikk has also suited up. He'll go as far as the Room's door and wait there—not the best assignment, especially for a young diver. But if Mikk doesn't know patience by now, he'll never learn it. And he swears he understands how long he might have to monitor that door.

Roderick anchors the skip to the remaining wall so that he won't have to use thrust in the small space. He and I will wait on board and will monitor everything through the suit cameras that Karl and Mikk will wear. They'll also have audio in their headpieces.

The dive will follow a strict schedule. Because Karl doesn't have a lot of distance to traverse between the skip and the Room's door, we decided on a two-hour dive—longer than I would have liked, and shorter than he wanted.

It'll only take him five minutes to get inside and, theoretically, five minutes to get back. The rest of the time, he should be observing and mapping.

Provided his equipment works inside. To our knowledge, no one has filmed the interior of the Room, and we don't know if that's because they haven't thought of it or if they didn't succeed when they tried.

Just before he puts on his headpiece, he attaches the device to his belt. Since we don't know much about how the device works, we don't want it inside his suit. We want to give him as much protection as possible.

Then he slips on his headpiece. It's as cautious as the rest of his suit—seven layers of protection, each with a different function including double night vision, and computerized monitors layered throughout the external cover. He hands me the handheld, which will report everything the cameras on the side of his headpiece "see."

We are the least confident in the handheld. The shield device might disrupt the signals the cameras send back. We tested as best we could near the *Business* and didn't have any trouble, but we're not sure if that was an accurate test.

Like so much with wreck diving, this part of the dive gets tested only in the field.

I'm nervous. Karl is not. Roderick hasn't said anything, and Mikk acts like this is a normal dive. While he's curious about the Room, it's an intellectual curiosity. He knows he won't be able to dive it this trip, so it's not the center of his attention.

In some ways, he's along for the ride, even more than I am.

We don't tether to the Room—that would be dangerous with the skip powered down—but we do extend a line. Karl is doing this as a courtesy to me. I won't dive without lines. I've seen too many divers get wreck blindness—they turn on their headlamps on a small space, they take a laser to the eyeball, their suit's visor malfunctions—and they can't get back without help.

The line is the simplest form of help. If they follow it from skip to wreck, then they know how to get back. We don't use lines inside wrecks, although I suggested it for the Room.

Karl gave that suggestion a lot of thought, and had an alteration. Once he reaches the door, he will attach a tether to one of the loops on his belt. If he loses consciousness in there, we can pull him back.

Mikk and Karl proceed to the airlock. They wave as they step inside.

They wait the required two minutes as their suits adjust. Then Mikk presses the hatch and Karl sends the lead out the door.

It only takes a moment to cleave to the jamb beside the Room's door. We picked that spot because it seemed soft enough to hold the line. Nothing else around the Room's exterior did.

They're stepping out of the airlock. They'll move at a very slow pace because they're good divers. They'll test the line. They'll make sure each part of their suits is functioning. Then they'll travel slowly to that door, and coordinate before Karl goes in.

I take those few minutes to walk into the cockpit. Roderick is sitting in what I consider to be my seat—the pilot's chair—and is already monitoring the readouts. In addition to the skip's cameras, some suit monitors send information directly to the skip itself. And both suits send heart-rates and breathing patterns—or will so long as nothing interferes with the signal.

I plug Karl's handheld into one small screen but only look at it to make sure the information is coming to me. Grainy flat images, mostly of the line, appear before me.

Then I look up. Roderick still has the portals opaqued.

"Let's watch this in real time," I say.

He doesn't look up from the instrumentation. "I don't like staring at interior station walls when I'm on a skip."

"I don't care," I say. "We have a team out there. We need our eyes as well as our equipment. We need every advantage we can get."

I shudder to think he's run dives in the habitats on instruments only, and make a mental note to tell Karl that night. It should be a requirement for each dive that the pilot watches from the cockpit. The pilot won't be able to see inside some of the spaces, but he will be able to see if there's a problem between the lead and the skip itself.

"Karl says I'm supposed to make the decisions," Roderick says.

"Well, I have twenty years of dive experience, and let me tell you, only amateurs let their people out of a ship on instrument only."

He winces, then flattens his hand against the control panel. With a hum, all of the windows become visible.

Usually being in the skip with the windows clear feels like you're inside a piece of black glass moving through open space. Right now, it seems like we've crashed into a junkyard. A blown wall opens to space on our left side. Beneath us, the habitat's floor is in shreds. Above us is the sturdy floor of the next level, and to our right is the line, leading to the Room's door.

Karl's already halfway down the lead. Mikk is hurrying to catch up.

I look at their breathing and heart rates. They're in the normal range. But it's not like Karl to move that fast.

I touch the communication panel. "You seeing something?"

"There's not a lot between the skip and the door, Boss." There's laughter in Karl's voice, as if he expected me to ask this question. "Relax."

I take my hand off the panel. Roderick is glaring at me, but in his expression I can see resignation. He knows that I'm going to run this skip while Karl's gone.

Roderick also knows he has no recourse. Even when Karl returns, telling on me won't make any difference. Karl won't ban me from these missions. If he does, I'll declare this entire trip a bust and leave. Then I'll return on my own or with a new team and dive it all again.

Karl reaches the door and tugs on the lead, checking its hold. It seems to be fine. Mikk arrives a moment later. His feet are curled beneath him, but they could just as easily brush against the floor.

This is the part of Mikk's dive that I would hate—floating there, waiting for Karl to do the actual work. For the first time since Karl changed our plans, I'm happy to be in the skip. At least I can pace here.

Karl runs a gloved hand along the door's edge. The cameras on his wrist light up and show what we saw on our preliminary dive—that the edges of this door are pockmarked—not from time or debris—but from people trying to break in. The metal is smoother here than anywhere else, as if countless people have run their gloved hands along the edges in the past.

"It's beautiful, isn't it?" my mother asks me through her suit. She turns her head toward me just a little, and I can see the outlines of her face through her headpiece. Behind her something hums.

Sweat has formed on my forehead. Goddamn Karl, he's right. I would have gotten lost in my own head, in my own memories, if I had gone in alone on this first trip.

I shake my head as if I can free it from the past and settle into the co-pilot's chair.

Karl pans the door, making sure nothing has changed since the last time we looked at it. Then his gloved hand slips down to the latch.

My breath catches as the door opens. The lights on his suit flare. He turns toward us, waves again, and then goes inside.

For a moment, I can see him outlined against the Room's darkness. Then he propels himself deeper and he is no longer visible through the clear windows of the skip.

The monitors show that his heart rate is slightly elevated. His breathing is rapid, but not enough to cut the dive short. This is the kind of breathing that comes from excitement and eagerness, not from panic or the gids.

"My God," he says. "This place is beautiful."

"It's even prettier inside," my mother says. Her voice sounds very far away. The lights blink against her suit, making her seem like she's covered in bright paint—all primary colors.

"You should see this," he says.

The cameras have fuzzed. We're not getting any visuals at all. The audio is faint.

"I don't like this," Roderick says as the instruments slowly fail.

I knew it would happen. Maybe I remembered something—or something in my subconscious recalled how faint my mother's voice had become. But I had known.

I had warned Karl and he said he was prepared.

But I'm cold. I'm sitting in the co-pilot's chair with my arms wrapped around my torso, feeling terrified.

My father said the device worked.

But what if it fails like the cameras fail?

Riya says a dozen others went in and came out. She showed me evidence.

Showed us evidence.

Karl made this choice.

"I don't like this at all." Roderick's hands are flying across the board, trying to bring up the readings. I glance at the handheld screen. The image is still there, faint and reassuring. Just a blur in all the fuzz.

Karl is moving forward.

But I know better than to tell Roderick everything will be all right. I glance at Mikk through the clear porthole.

He's holding the lead and waiting, just like he's supposed to. And good man that he is, he isn't even peering in the door.

He's following orders to the letter.

Static, a buzz, and a harmonic. A voice? I can't tell. Roderick is still working the instrument panel and I'm staring through the window at the door beyond.

All I see is blackness.

Karl is probably seeing lights. Hearing voices in harmony. Listening to the blend.

I hope the device protects him.

My arms tighten. My stomach aches. I feel ill.

I catch myself about to curse Karl for being right about my reactions. But I'm superstitious. I can't curse him. Not now. Not while we're waiting for him to come out of that Room.

12

We wait for an hour. Then an hour and a half.

Then two.

At two hours ten minutes, Mikk asks, "Should I reel him in?"

We haven't had any contact. We don't have any readings.

Karl is the kind of diver who never wastes a second, the kind who is always on time.

"How much oxygen does he have without the refills?" I ask Roderick.

"Five, maybe six hours, so long as he's breathing right. He didn't think he needed the larger storage, since the skip was so close."

I would have made the same judgment. My suit can handle two weights of oxygen as well. The back-ups are in case the internal supply gets compromised somehow, not as supplements to it.

"You want to wait another hour?" Roderick asks. No more pretense at being in charge. We both know I'm the one qualified to make the right decisions.

And oddly, as cold as I am, I'm calm. The emotions I felt at the beginning of the dive are long gone.

It's the two younger members of the team who are beginning to panic.

And that's reason enough to bring Karl in.

"Tug," I say to Mikk. "See if he responds."

Mikk tugs and then grunts as if in surprise. The tether attached to Karl has gone slack.

Roderick looks at me, terrified. Mikk says, "What do I do?"

We have to know the severity of this.

"One more gentle tug," I say. Maybe Karl has let out the line. Maybe he's closer than we think.

Mikk tugs again. I can see how little effort he uses, how his movement should just echo through the tether.

Instead it comes careening back at him, with something attached.

Something small and U-shaped.

"Oh, no," Mikk says.

And I hear the same words come out of my mouth as I realize what I'm seeing.

"What is it?" Roderick asks, his voice tight with fear.

"Karl's belt," I say. "The tug dislodged Karl's belt."

***

ONLY, IT TURNS OUT, MY ASSESSMENT ISN'T ENTIRELY accurate. The tug didn't dislodge Karl's belt.

Karl did. He unlatched it. There's no way to tell how long ago he did so either.

He got disoriented or lost or maybe he was reaching for the tether to pull himself back. Whatever happened, his fingers found the controls holding the belt to his suit and unhooked it.

Mikk shows us the seal with his own cameras, how it's unhooked in such a way that only the suit-wearer could have done. It didn't break and it didn't fall off.

Karl let it go.

"So pretty," my mother says, her voice a thread. "So very pretty."

"Pan it for me," I say, forcing the memory of my mother aside.

Mikk does. The knife is in its holder. So are the backup breathers.

And the device.

Mikk grabs it as I realize what I'm seeing. "I'm going after him," Mikk says, attaching the device to his belt.

"*No*," I say with great force. "You are staying put."

"But we need to get him. He can't be that far in. The tether didn't come back from a great distance."

"I know," I say. "But going in disoriented him, and he's got more experience than you. It'll disorient you. I'm going in."

"He said you're not supposed to dive." Roderick has put his hand on my arm.

I shake it off.

"I've been in there before," I say. "I know what to expect. Neither of you do. Mikk is strong enough to get me out if he has to. We'll double-tether me. We'll hook to my belt and my suit. He'll be able to pull us free."

"Karl says if you lose one diver, you shouldn't send another after him." Roderick is speaking softly. He thinks he's not being overheard, but I have the communications panel lit.

"That's if the other person's dead or dying," I say. "For all we know, he's wreck blind and lost. You want him to float around in there?"

"Can he survive without this device thing?" Mikk asks.

Roderick starts at Mikk's voice, then frowns at me.

"I did," I say. "I didn't have a shield. People do survive the Room without protection. The problem is that most folks don't even realize their companions are in trouble for hours. Maybe the Room doesn't kill them. Maybe the Room disorients them. Maybe, if that's what happens and if someone catches it soon enough, the other person gets out."

"Two point five hours," Mikk says, sounding breathless. "That's quick, isn't it?"

"Do you need to come into the skip?" I ask him as I grab my suit. I strip, not caring that Roderick is watching. I hate wearing the suit over my clothes. "You sound like you're short of air."

"I have plenty," Mikk says.

"You can recover while I'm getting suited," I say.

"His heart rate is elevated, but still in the safe zone," Roderick says. "But if you want to bring him in, then let's do it now."

Abort. Leave Karl. That's what Roderick is saying, in code now that he realizes Mikk—and maybe Karl himself—is listening.

"Stay there," I say. "I'm coming to you."

I have to slow down. I need to dress properly, make sure my suit functions. My own heart rate is elevated, and I'm trying not to listen to the low hum that's been haunting the back of my brain since that damn door opened.

My suit is thinner than Karl's. Body-tight with fewer redundant controls. I used to think he was too cautious. Now I wish I had all the equipment he did.

I check systems, then put on my head gear. I don't bother with extra cameras, although I don't tell Roderick that. I slide on my gloves, grab five tethers, and sling them along my belt hook like rolled up whips.

I open the airlock and look directly at Roderick. "Now you're in charge," I say as I let the door close.

The two minutes it takes for my suit to adjust seem like five hours. I work on slowing my own breathing, making sure I'm as calm as I can be.

Then I press open the exterior door.

My suit immediately gives me the temperature and notes the lack of atmosphere. It warns me about some small floating debris.

I place my hand on the lead and slide toward Mikk. I can see his face through his headgear.

He looks terrified.

Now I wish we hadn't brought one of the strong divers. I would give anything for someone with a lot of experience.

But I don't have that.

I have the children.

And I have to make the most of them.

13

MIKK ATTACHES TETHERS TO MY BELT, MY SUIT AND ONE of my boots. I must look like some kind of puppet. I warn him not to tug for at least an hour, unless I tug first. I take the device, turn it off, then turn it on, and make sure the lights run along the bottom and sides like they're supposed to.

They do.

I attach it to my belt.

Then I float toward that damn door.

The opening looks smaller than I remember and somewhat ordinary. In my career, I'd gone through countless doors that led to an inky blackness, a blackness that would eventually resolve itself under the lights of my suit.

But right now, I have those lights off. I want to see the interior as I remember it. I want to see the light show.

Only I don't. There are no lights. The persistent hum that I'd been hearing since we arrived has grown.

It sounds like the bass line to a cantata. I freeze near the door and listen. First the bass, then the tenors, followed by altos, mezzo sopranos, and sopranos. Voices blending and harmonizing.

Only they aren't. What I had identified years ago as the voices of the lost is actually some kind of machine noise. I can hear frequency and pitch, and my mind assembled those sounds—or to be more accurate, those vibrations—into music, which as a child was something I could understand.

Now I understand what I'm hearing and for the first time since I go into the Room, I'm nervous.

"Your heart rate is elevated," Roderick says from the control room.

"Copy that," I say, and flick on my suit lights. They illuminate everything around me. There's a floor, a ceiling, the window that we'd already observed, and walls.

A completely empty room.

Except for Karl, floating free in the middle of it. His face is tilted toward the floor, his legs bent, his feet raised slightly. Occasionally he bumps against something and changes trajectory.

He's either unconscious or—

I don't let myself complete that thought. I use a nearby wall to propel myself toward him. I grab him by the waist and pull him toward me. His bulky suit is hard to hold; I undo the tether on my boot and attach it to his right wrist.

That's not normal procedure—you could pull off the arm of the suit if you're not careful—but I don't plan to let go of him. Instead, I tug my remaining tethers, and hope Mikk is strong enough to pull us both out.

It takes a moment, and then we're moving backwards. I shift slightly so that I can see if we're about to hit anything.

The empty room stuns me. I expected not just the lights, but shades of the people lost. Or their remains. Or maybe just a few items that they had brought in with them, things that had fallen off their suits and remained, floating in the zero gravity for all time.

The previous divers wearing the device said they couldn't recover Commander Trekov—that he wouldn't leave. Were they lying? Or had they seen something I hadn't?

The open door looms. I kick away from the wall and float a little too high. I have to let go of Karl with one hand to push away from the ceiling.

Then we slide through the door and into the destroyed habitat. Mikk still clings to the tethers.

I shove Karl at him, then reach behind me and grab that damn door.

It takes all of my strength to close it. There's some kind of resistance—something that makes the movement so difficult that I can't do it on my own.

I'm not going to ask Mikk for help, though, and I'm not going to leave the door open. I grunt and shove, then turn on the gravity in boots for leverage. I sink to the metal floor, brace my feet, and push that door.

It takes forever to close. I'm sweating as I do, and my suit is making little beeping noises, warning me about the extreme exertion. Roderick is cautioning me, and Mikk is telling me to wait so that he can help.

I don't wait.

The door closes and I lean on it, wondering how I can close it permanently, so no one ever goes in there again.

I can't come up with anything—at least, not something I can do fast—so I make sure it's latched, and then I turn off the gravity in my boots. As I float upwards, I grab the lead.

I wrap my other hand around Karl and pull him with me. Mikk is protesting, repeating over and over again that he can bring Karl in.

Of course, Mikk can bring him in, but he won't. I'm the one who brought Karl here. I'm the one who put him in charge. I'm the one who didn't protest when he wanted to go into that Room alone.

He's my responsibility, and I need to get him back to the skip.

It only takes a few minutes. It's not hard to move him along. Mikk moves ahead of us and pulls open the skip's exterior door. Together we shove Karl into the airlock and then follow him inside.

I detach the lead. As I close the exterior door, I hear Mikk gasp.

I turn.

His body is visibly trembling. He's looking into Karl's faceplate.

I walk over to them and look.

Karl's face has shrunken in on itself. His eyes are gone, black holes in what was once a handsome face.

"He's dead," Mikk says and he sounds surprised.

That's when I realize I'm not. I think I knew Karl was dead when his belt appeared at that door. Karl's too cautious to lose his extra breathers, his weapons, and the device.

"What happened to him?" Roderick asks from inside the skip.

I touch Karl's faceplate. It's scratched, cloudy, marred by the passage of time. The suit is so fragile that my grip has loosened its exterior coating.

He didn't just die. He suffocated. Or froze. Or both. His suit ran out of oxygen. The environmental systems shut off, and he was left to the blackness of space as if he were outside the station, unprotected.

"Is it something catching?" Roderick's voice rises.

"No," I say. At least, not yet. Someday we'll all die from the passage of time.

"Then what is it?" Roderick asks. I realize at that moment, he's not going to open the interior door until I tell him.

"The device malfunctioned," I say, and that's true. It didn't protect him, although it protected me. "The Room killed him."

"How?" Mikk asks, his voice nearly a whisper.

All I have is a working theory at the moment, and I learned long ago not to let others know my theories. It causes problems, particularly if I'm right.

"I don't know exactly how," I say, and that's not entirely a lie. I don't know the mechanics of what happened exactly, although I do know what caused it.

That Room has a functioning stealth system. Ancient stealth, not the stuff we invented. The kind we found on the Dignity Vessel. Only here, it works, and has continued to work over time.

That's why we couldn't find an energy signal, like we did on the Dignity Vessel. Because the stealth tech is working here, masking everything, including itself.

The station isn't growing. The stealth shield is degrading. The exterior parts of the station move in a slower timeframe. The interior part, nearest the stealth tech itself, is moving at an accelerated pace.

That's why Karl died when the device malfunctioned. Time accelerated for him.

I wonder if that was when he saw the lights. Time passing, things appearing and changing, like the light from stars long gone, seen over a distance.

At least he hadn't died frightened.

Or had he? Thinking he was alone in that big empty Room.

Thinking we had abandoned him.

Like all the other souls lost in that horrible place.

14

We get him inside. It's harder in real gravity; he's heavier than I expected. Roderick and Mikk want to remove the suit, to see what really happened, but I talk them out of it.

We'll do it on the *Business.*

We fill out logs, download information, remove equipment—all the things you're supposed to do at the end of a dive. We do it without speaking, and while trying not to look at the body on the floor behind us.

Then Roderick goes to the cockpit. Mikk sinks down beside Karl, as if staring at him would bring him back. I take out the device. It's still on. The lights run along the bottom in the same pattern they did when I picked it up from Mikk.

I shut it off again, then turn it on. I can feel no vibration, nothing to signal that the thing is working. Nothing changes around me—no visual shift, no audio hallucination.

Nothing.

Just like before.

I should have seen that as a warning.

But I didn't.

It was my fault for trusting technology I didn't understand.

15

MOMENTS LATER, THE SKIP ARRIVES AT THE *BUSINESS*. Roderick sends the signal and we ease into the docking bay. The doors shut behind us, and the countdown begins until the atmosphere inside the bay gets restored.

No one here knows that Karl is dead. No one knows how spectacularly we failed.

I tell Roderick and Mikk that Karl has to remain on the skip. We'll send in some of the other crew to retrieve him, while I look up the forms he filled out so that we would take care of his body according to his wishes.

I also tell them not to say much until we meet tonight in the lounge.

Then I take the device, tuck the handheld into my pocket, and leave the skip. I'm going to meet the team first and I'm going to tell them what went wrong.

My father and Riya are standing near the door. No one else is with them and I have the distinct impression they've prevented the rest of the team from coming here.

My father is smiling. Riya is looking hopeful. Somehow they know we were in the Room.

All of my good intentions fade.

I toss the device at them. "This damn thing malfunctioned."

It skitters across the floor. My father is staring at me. Riya bends down to pick it up. As she stands, she frowns.

"Obviously it didn't fail," she says. "You're here."

"*I'm* here," I say, "but Karl is dead."

"Karl?" Riya glances at my father as if he understands what I'm talking about.

And to his credit, he does. "You let Karl go into the Room?"

"I didn't let him do anything," I snap. "He's in charge."

Or he *was* in charge. But I don't correct myself.

"He chose to go in. He decided last night."

"You let him?" my father repeated.

Behind me, I can hear the door to the skip snap shut. Footsteps along the floor tell me that Roderick and Mikk have joined us, but have stopped just a few meters back.

"How irresponsible of you." Riya shakes her head. "I gave this to you with the express understanding that you would use it."

"Really?" I say. "You gave it to me so someone could access that Room and recover your father, which isn't possible by the way."

"You were supposed to go. That's the basis for our agreement." She's still shaking the device at me. "You were supposed to go."

She didn't react to what I said about her father. Maybe she hadn't understood me.

"What you want," I say slowly, as if I'm talking to a child, "is not possible. Your father is not recoverable. Didn't the previous people who went in tell you that? Didn't they tell you how empty that fucking Room is?"

"It's not our responsibility that he died," she says. "You didn't follow my instructions."

I know she heard me the second time. And it's clear she doesn't care. She knew what was in that Room. She knew that her father—or some kind of ghost of him—wasn't there.

I snatch the device from her hand. "What happens if I break this thing?"

"Don't," my father says, but he's not scared. He is looking at my face, not at the device in my hand.

I turn and toss it to Mikk. He catches it, looking surprised. He holds it like it burns him, even though it's cool to the touch.

Then I advance on my father. "Tell me what's really going on here."

"You were supposed to go in," he says.

"I did," I say. "I went in and recovered my friend."

"He's like almost mummified," Roderick says, his voice shaking. "What does that?"

My father looks at me, then looks at Riya. She is staring at Roderick.

"They both went in?" she asks. "Together?"

"The boss already told you," Mikk says. "She had to recover his body. He went in alone. It was a smart dive move.

He was going to map everything. He thought he'd be clearer headed than everyone else."

"You shouldn't have allowed it," my father says.

"Maybe if I'd had all the information, I wouldn't have," I say. "What aren't you two telling me? Besides the fact that you knew the Room was empty."

"It's not our fault," Riya says. "You didn't listen."

"I listened," I say. "You wanted us to recover your father. You wanted me to treat it like I would treat any other wreck, and your father would be salvage. That's what you offered. You came to me because I'd gotten out of the Room before and you figured I wouldn't be scared to wear the device…"

My voice trails off as I listen to what I had just said. *I had gotten out of the Room before*. That's why they hired me. Not because of the device. Not because of her father.

Because I had escaped once before.

"The device doesn't work, does it?" I ask. "It's just pretty lights and nothing more."

"No," my father says, but Mikk takes the device and rips it apart. He takes out the center piece, the part I couldn't quite place, and stomps on it.

The lights still run along the outer edge of the frame.

"Son of a bitch," he says.

Roderick takes the device, turns it over, then crouches and looks at the pieces on the floor of the bay. Whatever that circle piece was, it was solid. There were no component parts, nothing that built into an engine or a chip.

"What were you people thinking?" he asks my father and Riya. "Why did you do this?"

"You were testing something else, weren't you?" I'm looking at my father. "This is something to do with your business, not with Mother, isn't it?"

He doesn't answer. He takes a step back. His cheeks flush.

"The others who went in, the ones you say tested the device, they're all survivors too, aren't they?" I ask.

Riya looks at my father again.

"I thought I was the only one still alive," I say.

My father is staring at me.

"But there are others, aren't there? And you found them. You sent them in. And they came out again. Didn't they?"

I take a step toward Riya and I let her see how angry I really am.

"Didn't they?" I ask again.

"Yes," she says.

"With a fake device. A handful of us can come and go as we please, can't we?"

"Yes," my father says.

"Why didn't you just tell us?" I ask.

"Would you have gone in then?" Riya asks.

"What does my getting into that Room prove?"

"That some of us can do it," my father says. "Some of us are designed to survive."

He clings to me. His helmet hits mine, and a crack appears along my visor. He covers it with his gloved hand and I can hear his voice in our comm system: Hurry, hurry, I think her suit is compromised.

He holds me so tight I can't breathe. We go through the door back to the single ship someone has brought and they stuff me inside. My dad can barely fit beside me. He checks the environmental system in the single ship, then pulls off my helmet and shoves a breather in my mouth.

C'mon, baby, c'mon, *he says,* don't die on me now.

My lungs hurt. My body aches. I look up at him and he's terrified. He keeps glancing out the porthole at the Room.

I had no idea, *he says.* I didn't know or I wouldn't have let her go in there. I certainly wouldn't have let her bring you.

But I can't think about it. I can't think about any of it. The hum is too loud, the voices echoing in my head. I close my eyes, and I refuse to think about it. About the way she stopped talking, the way her hand slipped from mine, the way her faceplate shattered as her body slammed into the wall.

Then I wrapped my arms around my knees, waiting. My daddy would come. I knew he would come.

I stayed there for what seemed like days, listening to the voices, feeling my mother's body brush against mine, as she got older and thinner and more and more horrible.

Finally I couldn't look any more. I closed my eyes and wondered when the voices would get me.

Then my father grabbed me and pulled me out.

And I was safe.

I look at him now. His eyes are wide. He has made a verbal slip and he knows it.

"My God," I say. "You know what's in there."

"Honey," my father says. "Don't."

I turn to Roderick and Mikk. "Go get the others. Bring a stretcher so that we can take Karl out of here with some dignity."

"I don't think we should leave you here," Mikk says. He's catching onto this quicker than Roderick.

"I'll be fine," I say. "Just hurry back."

They head to the door. Riya watches them go. My father keeps looking at me.

"You tell me what you know," I say, "Or I'm going to have the authorities come get both of you for fraud and murder. You clearly brought us out here on false pretenses, and now a man is dead."

Karl is dead. My heart aches.

"Call them," Riya says. "They won't care. Our contract is with them."

My father closes his eyes.

I look from him to her. "For stealth tech. This is all about stealth tech."

"That's right," she says. "You're one of the lucky few who can work in its fields without risks."

Lucky few. Me and a handful of others, all of whom were conned by this woman and my father. For what? A government military contract?

"What are you trying to do?" I ask. "Consign us to some government hell hole?"

My father has opened his eyes. He's shaking his head.

"No, you're just the test subjects," Riya says, apparently oblivious to my tone. "Before they approved our project, they wanted to make sure everyone who got out before could get out again. You were the last one. Your father didn't think you would work with us, but I proved him wrong."

"I signed on to help you recover your father," I say to her.

She shrugs one shoulder. "I never knew him. I really don't care about him. And you were right. I already knew he wasn't in that Room. But I figured telling you about him would work. I'm not the only one in this bay who was abandoned by her father."

My father puts a hand to his forehead. I haven't moved.

"I thought this was an historical project," I say, maybe too defensively. "I thought this was a job, like the kind I used to do."

"That's what you were supposed to think," she says. "Only you weren't supposed to send someone else into the Room. You're the only one with the marker."

Marker. As in genetic marker. I turn to my father.

"That's what you meant by designed. I'm some kind of test subject. I have some kind of genetic modification.,"

"No," he says. "Or yes. Or I'm not sure. You see, we think that anyone on a Dignity Vessel had been bred or genetically modified to work around stealth tech. Then the ships got stranded and the Dignity crews mingled with the rest of the population. Some of us have the marker. You do. I do. Your mother didn't."

He says that last with some pain. He still grieves her. I don't doubt that. But somehow he got mixed up in this.

"There were no Dignity Vessels this far out," I say. "They weren't designed to travel huge distances, and they weren't manufactured outside of Earth's solar system."

"Don't insult my intelligence," he says. "We know you found a Dignity Vessel a few years ago. I've seen it."

Because I salvaged it and got paid for it. I couldn't leave it in space, a deathtrap to whoever else wandered close to it.

Like this Room is.

I salvaged the vessel and gave it to the government so they could study the damn stealth tech.

And now my father has seen the vessel.

"That's how I knew how to find you," he says.

"You didn't need me," I say. "You had the others."

"We needed all of you," Riya says. "The government won't give us a go unless we had a one-hundred percent success rate. Which we do. Your friend Karl simply proves that you need the marker or you're subject to the interdimensional field."

Karl and Junior and my mother and who knows how many others.

"How long have the government known?" I ask. "How long have they known that the Room is a stealth-tech generator?"

She shrugs. "Why does it matter?"

"Because they should have shut it down." I'm even closer to her than I was before. She's backing away from me.

"They can't," my father says. "They don't know how."

"Then they should have blocked off the station," I say. "This place is dangerous."

"There are centuries' worth of warnings to keep people away," Riya says. "Besides, it's not our concern. We have scientists who can replicate that marker. We think we've finally discovered a way to work with real stealth tech. Do you know what that's worth?"

"My life, apparently," I say. "And my mother's. And Karl's."

Riya is looking at me. She's finally understanding how angry I am.

"Don't," my father says.

"Don't what?" I ask. "Don't hurt her? Why should you care? I could have died in there. Me, the daughter you swore to protect. Or did you abandon that oath along with your search for my mother? Was that even real?"

"It was real, honey," he says. "That's how I found this. Riya and I met at a survivor's meeting. We started talking—"

"*I don't care!*" I snap. "Don't you understand what you've done?"

"You wouldn't have died," he says. "That's why we approached you last. Once we were sure the others made it, then we came to you. Besides, you've done much more dangerous things on your own."

"And so has Karl." I'm close to both of them now. I'm so angry, I'm trembling. "But you know what the difference is?"

My father shakes his head. Riya watches me as if she's suddenly realized how dangerous I can be.

"The difference is that we chose to take those risks," I say. "We didn't choose this one."

"I heard you tell the team," Riya says, "that someone might die on this mission."

"I always tell my teams that," I say. "It makes them vigilant."

"But this time you believed it," my father says.

"Yeah," I say softly. "I thought that someone would be me."

16

And that's the crux of it. I know it as soon as I say it. I thought I would die on this mission and apparently, I was fine with that.

I thought I'd die in multicolored lights and song, like I thought my mother had died, and I thought it a beautiful way to go. I'd even convinced myself that I would die diving, so it would be all right.

I would be done.

But it's not all right. Karl's dead, and I can't even prove fault, except my own. Only when I review the decisions we made, we made the right ones with the information we had.

The thought brings me up short, prevents me from slamming Riya or my father against the bay wall.

Somehow I get out of that bay without either of them.

I don't speak to them as the *Business* leaves the station. I don't speak to them when I drop them at the nearest outpost. I expressly tell them that if they contact me or my people again, I will find a way to hurt them—but I don't know exactly how I would do that.

Riya's right. The government would back them because they're working on a secret and important project. Stealth tech is the holy grail of military research. So she and my father can get away with anything.

And—stupid me—I finally realize that my father has no feelings for me at all. He never has. The clinging I remember is just him pulling me free of the Room, leaving my mother—my poor mother—behind.

I can't even guarantee that we weren't part of some early experiment on the same project. While my father was telling my mother's parents to care for me while he tried to recover her, he might have been simply trying to recoup his losses from that trip, experimenting with people and markers and things that survive in the strangest of interdimensional fields.

After we leave my father and Riya on the outpost, we have a memorial service for Karl. I talk the longest because I knew him the best, and I don't cry until we send him out into the darkness, still in his suit with his knife and breathers.

He would have wanted those. He would have appreciated the caution, even though it was caution—in the end—that got him killed.

As we head back to Longbow Station, I have decided to resuscitate my business. Only I'm not going to wreck dive like I used to. I'm going to find Dignity Vessels. I'm going to capture anything that vaguely resembles stealth tech and I'm going to find a place to keep it where our government can't get it.

I'm going to run a shadow project. I'm going to find out how this stuff works and I'm going to do it before the government does because I won't have to follow the regulations.

The government and the people like my father, they have to follow certain rules and protocols, all the while keeping the project secret.

I won't have to. If I go far enough out of the sector, I won't have to follow any rules at all.

I can make my own. Change the way the battle is fought. Redefine the war.

I learned that from Ewing Trekov. Don't fight the war you're given; fight the war you can envision.

Once the government has stealth tech, they'll have a seemingly invincible military. They'll be stronger in ways that can hurt the smaller governments in the region and anyone who works at the edges of the law, like I do.

But if we have stealth tech too, then all sides are equal. And if we can figure out how to use that tech in ways they haven't imagined, then we get ahead.

All my life, I searched the past for my purpose. I sensed that something back there opened the key to my future.

Who knew that I would find all that I lost in the one place that had taken everything from me.

There are no souls in that Room, just like there are no voices.

There's only the harshness of time.

And like the ancients before me, I'm going to harness that harshness into a weapon, a defense, and a future.

I don't know what I'm going to do with it.

Maybe I'll just wait, and let the future reveal itself like the habitats on the station, one small section at a time.

ABOUT THE AUTHOR

INTERNATIONAL BESTSELLING WRITER Kristine Kathryn Rusch has won two Hugo awards, a World Fantasy Award, and six *Asimov's* Readers Choice Awards. For more information about her work, please go to kristinekathrynrusch.com. For more information about the Diving universe, to which this story belongs, go to divingintothewreck.com.

Also by

Kristine Kathryn Rusch

Alien Influences
The End of The World (novella)
The Retrieval Artist Series

The Diving Universe:

Novellas

Diving into the Wreck
The Room of Lost Souls
Becalmed
Becoming One with the Ghosts
Stealth
Strangers at the Room of Lost Souls
The Spires of Denon

Novels

Diving into the Wreck
City of Ruins
Boneyards
The Diving Omnibus, Volume One
Skirmishes (September 2013)

CPSIA information can be obtained at www.ICGtesting.com
Printed in the USA
LVOW06s1530031215

465220LV00001B/75/P